WHITE

'In *White Butterfly* . . . good-time girls, corrupt politicians, trigger-happy psychopaths and other crime novel fixtures are all in place. But Walter Mosley's writing hums with the particular rhythms and blues of the black American experience. What makes these books special is their vivid portrayal of life in the side streets where Philip Marlowe seldom ventured' *Time*

'A hypnotic, unpredictable, and serious storyteller' *Entertainment Weekly*

. . . and for A Red Death:

'This novel is so hot it burns your fingers with blistering dialogue and multi-coloured images. Highly addictive food' *Evening Standard*

'I have been waiting for someone like Walter Mosley for a very long time. It's been worth the wait, for at last here is a successor to Chester Himes' *City Limits*

'Mosley's second novel confirms him as one of crime writing's finds of the 1990s' *Mike Ripley, Daily Telegraph*

. . . and for Devil in a Blue Dress:

'A magnificent first novel by Walter Mosley in which, from the first page, it's clear we have discovered a wonderful new talent . . . the most exciting arrival in the genre for years' *Financial Times*

'A first novel of astonishing virtuosity, upending Chandler's LA to show a dark side of a different kind' *Sunday Times*

'An original, beguiling creation. One of the most impressive first crime novels' *The Times*

Walter Mosley was born in Los Angeles in 1952
and now lives in New York.

white butterfly

WALTER MOSLEY

PAN BOOKS

First published 1992 by W. W. Norton & Company, Inc., New York

First published in Great Britain 1992 by Serpent's Tail

This edition published 1994 by Pan Books Limited
a division of Pan Macmillan Publishers Limited
25 Eccleston Place, London SW1W 9NF
and Basingstoke

Associated companies throughout the world

ISBN 0 330 33053 5

3 5 7 9 8 6 4

A CIP catalogue record for this book is available from
the British Library

Printed and bound in Great Britain

For the stories he keeps on telling,
I dedicate this book to Leroy Mosley.

ONE

"**E**ASY RAWLINS!" someone called.

I turned to see Quinten Naylor twist the handle of my front gate.

"Eathy," my baby, Edna, cooed as she played peacefully with her feet in her crib next to me on the front porch.

Quinten was normal in height but he was broad and powerful-looking. His hands were the size of potholders, even under the suit jacket his shoulders were round melons. Quinten was a brown man but there was a lot of red under the skin. It was almost as if he were rage-colored.

As Quinten strode across the lawn he crushed a patch of chives that I'd been growing for seven years.

The violent-colored man smiled at me. He held out his beefy paw and said, "Glad I caught you in."

"Uh-huh." I stepped down to meet him. I shook his hand and looked into his eyes.

When I didn't say anything there was an uncomfortable moment for the Los Angeles police sergeant. He stared up into my face wanting me to ask him why he was there. But all I wanted was for him to leave me to go back into my home with my wife and children.

"Is this your baby?" he asked. Quinten was from back east, he spoke like an educated white northerner.

"Yeah."

"Beautiful child."

"Yeah. She sure is."

"She sure is," Quinten repeated. "Takes after her mother, I bet."

"What do you want wit' me, officer?" I asked.

"I want you to come with me."

"I'm under arrest?"

"No. No, not at all, Mr. Rawlins."

I knew when he called me mister that the LAPD needed my services again. Every once in a while the law sent over one of their few black representatives to ask me to go into the places where they could never go. I was worth a precinct full of detectives when the cops needed the word in the ghetto.

"Then why should I wanna go anywhere wit' you? Here I am spendin' the day wit' my fam'ly. I don't need no Sunday drive wit' the cops."

"We need your help, Mr. Rawlins." Quinten was becoming visibly more crimson under his brown shell.

I wanted to stay home, to be with my wife, to make love to her later on. But something about Naylor's request kept me from turning him down. There was a kind of defeat in the policeman's plea. Defeat goes down hard with black people; it's our most common foe.

"Where we gonna go?"

"It's not far. Twelve blocks. Hundred and Tenth Street." He turned as he spoke and headed for the street.

I yelled into the house, "I'm goin' fo' a ride with Officer Naylor. I'll be back in a while."

"What?" Regina called from her ironing board out back.

"I'm goin' out for a while," I yelled. Then I waved at my forty-foot avocado tree.

Little Jesus peeked out from his perch up there and smiled.

"Come on down here," I said.

The little Mexican boy climbed down the tree and ran up to me with a silent smile stitched across his face. He had the face of an ancient American, dark and wise.

"I don't want you off exploring today, Jesus," I said. "Stay around here and look after your mother and Edna."

Jesus looked at his feet and nodded.

"Look up here at me." I did all the talking when around Jesus because he hadn't said a word in the eight years I'd known him.

Jesus squinted up at me.

"I want you close to home. Understand me?"

Quinten was at his car, looking at his watch.

Jesus nodded, looking me in the eye this time.

"All right." I rubbed his crew-cut peach fuzz and went out to meet the cop.

Officer Naylor drove me to an empty lot in the middle of the 1200 block of 110th Street. There was an ambulance parked out front, flanked by patrol cars. I noticed a bright patent-leather white pump in the gutter as we crossed the street.

A crowd had gathered on the sidewalk. Seven white police officers stood shoulder to shoulder across the front of the property, keeping everybody out. The feeling was festive. The policemen were all at ease, smoking cigarettes and joking with the Negro gawkers.

The lot itself was decorated with two rusted-out Buicks that were hunkered down on broken axles in the weeds. A knotty oak had died toward the back end of the lot.

Quinten and I walked through the crowd. There were men, women, and children stretching their necks and bobbing back and forth. A boy said, "Lloyd saw'er. She dead."

When we walked past the line of policemen one of them caught me by the arm and said, "Hey you, son."

Quinten gave him a hard stare and the officer said, "Oh, okay. You can go on."

Just one of the many white men I've shrugged off. His instinctive disrespect and arrogance hardly even mattered. I turned away and he was gone from my life.

"Right this way, Mr. Rawlins," Quinten Naylor said.

There were four plainclothes policemen looking down at the back of the tree. I couldn't make out what it was that they saw.

I recognized one of the cops. He was a burly white man, the kind of fat man who was fat everywhere, even in his face and hands.

"Mr. Rawlins," the burly man said. He held out a pillowy hand.

"You remember my partner," Quinten said. "Roland Hobbes."

We'd come around the tree by then. There was a woman in a pink party dress, a little open at the breast, sitting with her back against the trunk. Her legs were straight out in front of her, a little apart. Her head tilted to the side, away from me, and her hands were on either side of her thighs with the palms up. Her left foot sported a white pump, her right foot was bare.

I remember the softness and the underlying strength of Roland Hobbes' hand and the insect I saw perched on the woman's temple. I wondered why she didn't bat it away.

"Nice to see you," I was saying to Hobbes when I realized that the insect was a dried knot of blood.

When Roland let go of my hand he listed toward Quinten and said, "Same thing."

"Both?" Quinten asked.

Roland nodded.

The girl was young and pretty. It was hard for me to think that she was dead. It seemed as if she might get up from there any minute and smile and tell me her name.

Somebody whispered, "Third one."

TWO

THEY CARRIED THE body away on a stretcher when the photographers were through—police photographers, not newsmen. A black woman getting killed wasn't photograph material for the newspapers in 1956.

After that Quinten Naylor, Roland Hobbes, and I got into Naylor's Chevrolet. He was still driving a 1948 model. I imagined him on his days off, in short sleeves, slaving and struggling under the hood to keep that jalopy running.

"Don't they give you a car when you with the police?" I asked.

"They called me from home. I came straight here."

"Then why'ont you buy yourself a new car?"

I was sitting in the front seat. Roland Hobbes had gotten in the back. He was deferential kind of a person, always polite and correct; I didn't trust him worth a damn.

"I don't need a new car. This car is just fine," Naylor said.

I looked down at the ruptured vinyl seat between my thighs. The gold-colored foam rubber gushed forth under my weight.

We drove quite a ways down Central Avenue. That was before the general decline of the neighborhood. The streets were clean and the drunks were few. I counted fifteen churches between 110th Street and Florence Boulevard. At that corner was the Goodyear Rubber Plant. It was a vast field with two giant buildings far off to the northern end. There was also the hangar for the Goodyear Blimp there. Across the street sat a World gas station. World was a favorite hangout for Mexican hot-rodders and motorcycle enthusiasts who decorated their German machines with up to three hundred pounds of chrome piping and doodads.

Naylor drove to the gate of the Goodyear plant and flashed his badge at the guard. We drove to a large asphalt parking lot where hundreds of cars were parked neatly in rows like they were on sale. There were always cars parked there, because the Goodyear plant worked twenty-four hours a day, seven days a week.

"Let's take a walk," Naylor said.

I got out of the car with him. Hobbes stayed in the backseat. He picked up a *Jet* magazine that Naylor had back there and turned directly to the centerfold, the bathing-suit picture.

We walked out into the center of the grassy field. The sky was tending toward twilight. Every fourth or fifth car driving the boulevards had turned on their lights.

I didn't ask Quinten what we were doing. I knew it was something important for him to want to impress me with the fact that he could get onto that fancy lawn.

"You hear about Juliette LeRoi?" Quinten asked.

I had heard about her, her death, but I asked, "Who?"

"She was from French Guiana. Worked as a cocktail waitress for the Champagne Lounge."

"Yeah?" I prompted him.

"About a month ago she was killed. Throat cut. Raped too. They found her in a trash can on Slauson."

It was back-page news. TV and radio didn't cover it at all. But most colored people knew about it.

"Then there was Willa Scott. We found her tied to the pipes under a sink in an abandoned house on Hoover. She had her mouth taped shut and her skull caved in."

"Raped?"

"There was semen on her face. We don't know if that happened before or after she died. The last time she was seen was at the Black Irish."

I felt a knot in my gut.

"And now we have Bonita Edwards."

I was watching the field and the row of businesses beyond on Florence. The air darkened even as Naylor spoke. Lights twinkled on in the distance.

"That this girl's name?" I asked him. I was sorry I had come. I didn't want to care about these women. The rumors around the neighborhood were bad enough, but I could ignore rumors.

"Yes." Quinten nodded. "A *dancer,* another bar girl. Three party girls. So far."

The grass shifted from green to gray with the dusk.

I asked, "So why you talkin' t'me?"

"Juliette LeRoi had been in that can for two days before somebody called in the smell. Rigor mortis had set in. They didn't find the marks until after the news story was out."

My stomach let out a little groan.

"Willa Scott and Bonita Edwards had the same marks."

"What marks do you mean?"

Quinten darkened like the night. "Burns," he said. "Cigar burns on their, their breasts."

"So it's all the same man?" I asked. I thought of Regina and Edna. I wanted to get home, to make sure the doors were locked.

The policeman nodded. "We think so. He wants us to know he's doing it."

Quinten stared me in the eye. Behind him L.A. sizzled into a net of electric lights.

"What you lookin' at?" I dared him.

"We need you on this one, Easy. This one is bad."

"Just who do you mean when you say 'we'? Who is that? You and me? We gonna go'n hire somebody?"

"You know what I mean, Rawlins."

In my time I had done work for the numbers runners, church-goers, businessmen, and even the police. Somewhere along the line I had slipped into the role of a confidential agent who represented people when the law broke down. And the law broke down often enough to keep me busy. It even broke down for the cops sometimes.

The last time I worked with Naylor he needed me to lure a killer named Lark Reeves out of Tijuana.

Lark had been in an illegal crap game in Compton and was down twenty-five dollars to a slumming white boy named Chi-Chi MacDonald. When Chi-Chi asked for his money he was a little too cocky and Lark shot him in the face. The shooting wasn't unusual but the color line had been crossed and Quinten knew that he could make a case for a promotion if he could pull Lark in.

As a rule I will not run down a black man for the law. But when Quinten came to me I had a special need. It was a week before Regina and I were to be married, and her cousin Robert Henry was in jail for robbery.

Robert had argued with a market owner. He said that a quart of milk he'd bought had soured in the store. When the grocer called him a liar Robert just picked up a gallon jug and made for the door. The grocer grabbed Bob by the arm and called to the checker for help.

Bob said, "You got a friend, huh? That's okay, 'cause I got a knife."

It was the knife that put Bob in jail. They called it armed robbery.

Regina loved her cousin, so when Quinten came to me about Lark I made him an offer. I told him that I'd set up a special poker game down in Watts and get the word out to Lark. I knew that Lark couldn't resist a good game.

High-stakes poker put Lark in San Quentin. He never connected me with the cops who busted the game and dragged him off to be identified at the station.

Quinten got his promotion because the cops thought that he had his thumb on the pulse of the black community. But all he really had was me. Me and a few other Negroes who didn't mind playing dice with their lives.

But I had stopped taking those kind of chances after I got married. I wasn't a stool for the cops anymore.

"I don't know nuthin' 'bout no dead girls, man. Don't you think I'd come tell ya if I did? Don't you think I'd wanna stop somebody killin' Negro women? Why, I got me a pretty young wife at home right now . . ."

"She's all right."

"How do you know?" I felt the pulse in my temples.

"This man is killing good-time girls. He's not after a nurse."

"Regina works. She comes home from the hospital, sometimes at night. He could be stalkin' her."

"That's why I need your help, Easy."

I shook my head. "Uh-uh, man. I cain't help you. What could I do?"

My question threw Naylor. "Help us," he said feebly.

He was lost. He wanted me to tell him what to do because the police didn't know how to catch some murderer who didn't make sense to them. They knew what to do when a man killed his wife or when a loan shark took out a bad debt. They knew how to question witnesses, white witnesses. Even though Quinten Naylor was black he didn't have sympathy among the rough crowd in the Watts community; a crowd commonly called *the element*.

"What you got so far?" I asked, mostly because I felt sorry for him.

"Nothing. You know everything I know."

"You got some special unit workin' it?"

"No. Just me."

The cars passing on the distant streets buzzed in my ears like hungry mosquitoes.

"Three girls dead," I said. "An' you is all they could muster?"

"Hobbes is on it with me."

I shook my head, wishing I could shake the ground under my feet.

"I cain't help you, man," I said.

"Somebody's got to help. If they don't, who knows how many girls will die?"

"Maybe you' man'll just get tired, Quinten."

"You've got to help us, Easy."

"No I don't. You livin' in a fool's nightmare, Mr. Policeman. I can't help you. If I knew this man's name or if I knew somethin', anything. But it's the cops gotta gather up evidence. One man cain't do all that."

I could see the rage gathering in his arms and shoulders. But instead of hitting me Quinten Naylor turned away and stalked off toward the car. I ambled on behind, not wanting to walk with him. Quinten had the weight of the whole community on his shoulders. The black people didn't like him because he talked like a white man and he had a white man's job. The other policemen kept at a distance too. Some maniac was killing Negro women and Quinten was all alone. Nobody wanted to help him and the women continued to die.

"You with us, Easy?" Roland Hobbes said. He put his hand on my shoulder as Naylor stepped on the gas.

I kept my silence and Hobbes took his friendly hand back. I was in a hurry to get to my house. I felt bad about turning down the policeman. I felt miserable that young women would die. But there was nothing I could do. I had my own life to attend to—didn't I?

THREE

I ASKED NAYLOR to let me off at the corner, intending to walk the last few steps home. But instead I stood there looking around. Night was coming on and I imagined that people were scurrying for shelter from a storm that was about to explode around them.

Not everybody was in a hurry.

Rafael Gordon was running a shell game in front of the Avalon, a tiny bar down toward the end of my block. Zeppo, the half-Italian, half-Negro spastic, was standing watch at the corner. Zeppo, who was always in a writhing fit, couldn't finish a sentence but he could whistle louder than most horn players could blow.

I waved at Zeppo and he shimmied at me, grimacing

and winking. I tried to catch Rafael's eye but he was intent on the two rubes he'd snagged. Rafael was a short Negro, more gray in hue than he was brown. He was missing the greater portion of his front teeth and his left eye was dead in its socket. Rubes would look at Rafael and know that they could out-smart him. And maybe they thought they wouldn't have to pay even if they lost; Rafael didn't look like he could whip a poodle.

But Rafael Gordon carried a cork-hafted black iron fishing knife in his sleeve, and he always had a few feet of tempered steel chain in his pocket.

"Just show me where the red ball lands," he sang. "Just show me the red ball and two dollars. Double your money and howl tonight." He moved the fake walnut shells from side to side, lifting them at various times to show what was, and what wasn't.

A big man I'd never seen before pointed at a shell. I turned away and walked toward my home.

I was thinking about the dead party girl; about how she was killed with no reason except maybe how she looked or who she looked like. I shuddered at the memory of how natural she appeared. When a woman forgets that she's supposed to be pretty and on display she looks like that murdered girl did; just some-body who's tired and needs to rest.

That got me thinking about Regina and what she looked like. There was no comparison, of course. Regina was royal in her bearing. She never wore cheap shiny clothes or costume jew-elry. When she danced it was not in that herky-jerky way that most young women moved. Regina's dancing was fluid and graceful like a fish in water or a bird on air.

The memory of that dead girl hung around me. I made it down to my front gate and looked to see that Regina and Edna were okay in the living room, I could see them through the window, then I got into my car and headed out to Hooper Street.

Mofass had his real estate office on Hooper at that time. It was on the second floor of a two-story building. I owned the building, though nobody but Mofass knew that. The bottom floor was rented to a Negro bookstore that specialized in inspirational literature. Chester and Edwina Remy rented the place. Like all the tenants in my seven buildings, the Remys paid their rent to Mofass. He gave it to me sometime after that.

I knew Mofass would be in, because he worked late seven nights a week. All he ever did was work and smoke cigars.

The staircase that led to Mofass' door was exposed to the outside. It groaned and sagged as I made my way. Before I ever got to the door I could hear Mofass coughing.

I came in to find him crumpled over his maple desk, making a sound like an engine that won't turn over.

"I told ya to stop that smoking, Mofass. That cigar gonna kill you."

Mofass lifted his head. His jowly face made him resemble a bulldog. His pathetic gesture made him look even more canine. Tears from all that coughing fell from his rheumy eyes. He held the cigar out in front of his face and stared at it in terror. Then he smashed the black stogie in a clear glass ashtray and pushed himself upright in his swivel chair.

He stifled a cough and clenched his fists.

"How you doin'?" I asked.

"Fine," he whispered, and then he gagged on a cough.

I took the chair he had for clients and waited for any business he might have had to discuss. We'd known each other for many years. Maybe that's why I had two minds about Mofass' illness. On one hand I was always sorry to see a man in misery. But then again, Mofass was a coward who had betrayed me once. The only reason I hadn't killed him was that I hadn't proven to be a better man.

"What's goin' on?" I asked.

"Ain't nuthin' happenin' but the rent."

We both smiled at that.

"I guess that's okay," I said.

Mofass held up his hand for me to be quiet and took a porcelain jar from his desk. He unscrewed it, held it to his nose and mouth, and took a deep breath. The smell of camphor and menthol stung my nose.

"You hear 'bout the latest girl?" Mofass asked, his voice back from death's door.

"No, uh-uh."

"They found her on a Hundred and Tenth. Out near you. They said that there was nearly twenty cops out there."

"Yeah?"

"Good-time girls. Ain't havin' such a good time no more," he said. "Crazy man killin' young things. It's a shame."

Mofass pulled a cigar from his vest pocket. He was about to bite off the tip when he saw me staring. He put the death stick back and said, "Gonna be trouble fo'us."

"Trouble how?"

"Lotsa yo' young tenants these girls, man. Single girls or deserted ones. They got a baby and a job, and on Friday night they go out with they friends lookin' fo'a man."

"So what? You think whoever doin' this gonna kill all our renters?"

"Naw, naw. I ain't all that stupid. I might not got no college under my belt like you but I could see what's in front'a my nose just as good as the next man."

"An' what is that?"

"Georgette Wykers and Marie Purdue told me that they movin' in together—for' p'otection. They said that they could take care of their kids better an' be safe too. Course they only be payin' half the rent."

"So? What could I do about that?"

Mofass smiled. Grinned. I could see all the way back to his

last, gold-capped molar. When Mofass showed that kind of pleasure it meant that he had been successful where money was con-
cerned.

"You don't need to do nuthin', Mr. Rawlins. I told'em that
the rules didn't 'low no doublin' up. Then I told Georgette that if
she moved in with Marie, then Marie could th'ow her out 'cause
Georgette's name wouldn't be on the contract."

If Mofass made money on the day he died he would die a
happy man.

"Don't bother with it, man," I said. "Let them girls do what
they want. You know they's a thousand people comin' out here
ev'ry day. Somebody move out an' somebody else just move in."

Mofass shook his head sadly and slow. He couldn't take a
deep breath but he felt sorry for me. How could I be so stupid and
not bleed the whole world for a dollar and some change?

"You got anything else t'say, Mofass?"

"Them white men called again today."

A representative of a company called DeCampo Associates
had been calling Mofass about some property I owned in Compton. They'd offered to buy it twice; the last time for more than
twice what the land was worth.

"I don't wanna hear about it. If they want that property it
must be worth more than they wanna pay."

I walked over to the window, because I didn't want to argue
about it again. Mofass thought that I should sell the land because
there was a quick profit. He was good in business from day to
day, but Mofass didn't know how to plan for the future.

"They got another deal now," he said. "You wanna say no to
a hundred thousand dollars?"

Out the window I saw a little boy pulling a blue wagon past
a streetlamp. He had thick soda bottles in the wagon. Six or seven
of them. At most that was fourteen cents, enough for three candy-
bars, just about. The boy was brown with bare feet and short

pants and a striped T-shirt. He was deep in thought as he pulled that wagon. Maybe he was thinking about his spelling lesson from last week. Maybe he wondered at the right way to spell kangaroo. But I suspected that that boy was wondering how to get the one cent he needed to buy a third candy bar.

"A hundred thousand?"

"They wanna meet with you," Mofass rasped.

I heard him lighting a match and turned just in time to see him take his first drag.

"What is it they want from us, William?" Mofass' real name was William Wharton.

Mofass, taking on a conspiratorial tone, said, "The county gonna develop Willoughyby Place into a main road, a four-lane avenue."

I owned nine acres on one side of Willoughby. It came as part of a deal I made to find an old Japanese gardener's lost property.

"So what?" I asked.

"These men will lend you the money for development. Hundred thousand dollars and they take you for a partner."

"Cain't wait t'give me money, huh?"

"All you gotta do is give me the okay, Mr. Rawlins, an' I'll tell'em that the board done voted."

Whenever anybody wanted to do business with me they did it through Mofass. He represented the corporation I'd formed to do business. The *board* was a committee of one.

I had to laugh to myself. Here I was a woodchopper's son. A Negro and an orphan and from the south too. There was never a chance in hell that I'd ever see five thousand dollars but here I was being courted by white real estate men.

"Set up a meeting with them," I said. "I want to get a look at these men. But don't get yo' greedy hopes up, Willy, prob'ly won't nuthin' come from it."

Mofass grinned, breathing in smoke through his teeth.

FOUR

IT WAS A warm evening. I parked down toward the end of my block. Zeppo and Rafael were gone. The cardboard box that Rafael had used for his table was flattened on the sidewalk. A dollop of blood festooned by a cracked tooth adorned the curb. Somebody had learned a bitter lesson in Rafael Johnson's school of sleight-of-hand.

The drying blood made me think of the dead party girl again.

I still needed to be alone after all that had happened. So I decided to have a shot before I went back to my wife.

On the inside the Avalon was about the size of a walled-up display window. There was a bar and six stools—that's it. Rita Coe served bottled beer and drinks mixed with water or ice.

There was only one customer, a big man facing the wall and hunkered down over a pay phone at the end of the bar.

"What you doin' here, Easy Rawlins?" Rita was hard and small with beady eyes and thin lips.

"Whiskey was what I had in mind."

"I thought you didn't drink in no bar so close to your house?"

"Well, I will today."

"Why not?" the big man asked the phone. "I'm ready."

Rita poured my scotch into a bullet glass.

"How's Regina and the baby?" Rita asked.

"Fine, both fine."

She nodded and looked down at my hands. "You hear about them girls been gettin' killed?"

"Nuthin' but, seems like."

"You know, I'm scared to walk out to my car when I close up at night."

"You close up alone?" I asked her. But before she could answer the big man hung up the phone so hard that it gave out a brief ring of complaint.

Dupree Bouchard stood up and turned toward us—all six feet five inches of him. He saw me and then looked around as if he were searching for a back door. But the only door was the one I'd come through.

Dupree and I had been friends when we were younger men. One night he drank too much and passed out—leaving me and his girlfriend, Coretta, with nothing to hold but each other.

Maybe he heard our hushed cries through his alcoholic stupor. Or maybe he blamed me for her murder the next day.

"Hey, Dupree. How's Champion treatin' you?"

We'd both worked at Champion Aircraft ten years earlier. Dupree was a master machinist.

"They ain't no good up there, Easy. Every time you turn

around they got another rule to hold you up. And if you a niggah, they got two rules."

"That's true," I said. "That's true. Everywhere you go it's the same."

"It's better back down home. At least down south a colored brother won't stab you in the back." He looked me in the eye when he said that. Dupree could never prove that I had done anything with or to Coretta. He just knew that I was with them one night and then she was gone from him forever.

"I don't know, Dupree," I said. "There hasn't been all that many lynchings up here in L.A. County."

"You wanna drink, Dupree?" Rita asked.

The big man sat down, two stools away from me, and nodded to her.

"How's your wife?" I asked to get him talking about something brighter.

"She's okay. I work at Temple Hospital now," he said.

"Really? My wife works there. Regina."

"What she look like?"

"Dark-complected. Pretty and kind of slim. She works in maternity ward."

"What time she work?"

"Eight to five usually."

"Then I prob'ly ain't even seen'er. I only been there two months and I'm on the graveyard shift. They got me doin' laundry in the basement."

"You like it?"

"Yeah," he said bitterly. "Love it."

Dupree took the drink that Rita brought and downed it in one swallow. He slapped two quarters on the bar and said, "I gotta go."

He went past me and out the door, silent and sullen. I remembered how loud he had laughed that last night with Coretta and me. His laugh was like thunder in those days.

I wished I could take back what had happened to my friend, my part in his lifelong despair. I wished it but wishes don't count for much in flesh and blood.

"Andre Lavender," I said to Rita.

"Say what?"

"Andre. You know him?"

"Uh-uh."

"Gimme some paper."

I wrote Andre's name and phone number and said, "Call him and say that I'd like him to come by and see you to your car at night."

"He work for you?"

"I did him a favor once. Now he could help you."

"Do I gotta pay him?"

"Shot of whiskey do him just fine."

I pushed my glass closer to her and she filled it again.

Jesus was doing cartwheels across the lawn in the porch light. Little Edna kept herself upright by holding the bars of her crib. She laughed and sputtered at her mute brother. I came in the gate and picked up a football that was nestled in among the dahlia bushes along the fence. I whistled, then threw the ball just when Jesus turned to see me. He caught the football, held it in one hand, and waved to Edna as if he were beckoning her with the other. She rattled her baby bars, bounced on the balls of her feet, and yelled as loud as she could, "Akach yeeee!"

Jesus kicked the ball so hard that it crashed against the far link fence. The jangling of steel was a kind of music for city children.

"What's goin' on out here?" Regina was framed for a moment by the gray haze of the screen door. She came out on the porch and stood in front of our little girl as if protecting her. Edna let out a howl. She couldn't see Jesus and the yard past her mother's skirts.

"Aw, com'on, honey. She's okay," I said as I mounted the three stairs to the porch.

"He could miss a kick out there an' tear her head off!"

Edna let herself fall hard on her diapered bottom. Jesus climbed up into the avocado tree.

"You got to be more careful, Easy," my wife of two years said.

"Eathy," echoed Edna.

I found it hard to answer, because it was always hard for me to think when looking at Regina. Her skin was the color of waxed ebony and her large almond-shaped eyes were a half an inch too far apart. She was tall and slender but, for all that she was beautiful, it was something else that got to me. Her face had no imperfection that I could see. No blemish or wrinkle. Never a pimple or mole or some stray hair that might have grown out of the side of her jaw. Her eyes would close now and then but never blink as normal people do. Regina was perfect in every way. She knew how to walk and how to sit down. But she was never flustered by a lewd comment or shocked by poverty.

I fell in love with Regina Riles each time I looked at her. I fell in love with her before we ever exchanged words.

"I thought it was okay, honey." I reached for her unconsciously and she moved away, a graceful dancer.

"Listen, Easy. Jesus don't know how to think about what's right for Edna. You got to do that for him."

"He knows more than you think, baby. He's been around

little children more than most women have. And he understands even if he doesn't talk."

Regina shook her head. "He got problems, Easy. You sayin' that he's okay don't make it so."

Jesus climbed down out of the tree and went to the side of the house to get into his room.

"I don't know what you mean, honey," I said. "Everybody got problems. How you handle your problems means what kinda man you gonna be."

"He ain't no man. Jesus is just a little boy. I don't know what kind of trouble he's had but I do know that it's too much for him, that's why he can't talk."

I let it drop there. I could never bring myself to tell her the real story. About how I rescued the boy from a missing woman's house after he had been bought and abused by an evil man. How could I explain that the man who mistreated Jesus had been murdered and I knew who'd done it, but kept quiet?

Regina hoisted Edna into her arms. The baby screamed. I wanted to grab them both and hug them so hard that all this upset would squeeze out.

Talking to Regina was painful for me sometimes. She was so sure about what was right and what wasn't. She could get me stirred up inside. So much so that sometimes I didn't know if I was feeling rage or love.

I waited outside for a moment after they went in, looking at my house. There were so many secrets I carried and so many broken lives I'd shared. Regina and Edna had no part of that, and I swore to myself that they never would.

I went in finally, feeling like a shadow, stalking himself into light.

FIVE

"**Y**OU BEEN DRINKIN'," Regina said when I walked through the door. I didn't think she could smell it and I hadn't had enough to stagger. Regina just knew me. I liked that, it made my heart kind of wild.

Edna and Regina were both on the couch. When the baby saw me she said, "Eathy," and pulled away to crawl in my direction. Regina grabbed her before she fell to the floor.

Edna hollered as if she had been slapped.

"You been down to the police station?"

"Quinten Naylor wanted to talk with me." I always felt bad when the baby cried. I felt that something had to be done before we could go on. But Regina just held her and talked to me as if there were no yelling.

"Then why you come home all liquored up?"

"Com'on, baby," I said. Everything seemed slow. I felt that there was more than enough time to explain to her, to calm everything down. If only Edna would stop crying, I thought, everything would be okay. "I just took a drink down at the Avalon."

"Musta been a long swallow."

"Yeah, yeah. I needed a drink after what Officer Naylor showed me."

That got her attention, but her stare was still hard and cold.

"He took me over to a vacant lot on a Hundred and Tenth. Dead girl over there. Shot-in-the-head dead. It's the same man killed them other two girls."

"They know who did it?"

I had to suppress my smile. Taking that angry glare off her face made me want to dance.

"Naw," I said, as soberly as I could.

"Then how do they know it's the same man?"

"He crazy, that's why. He marks 'em with a hot cigar."

"Rape?" she asked in a small voice. Edna stopped crying and looked at me with her mother's questioning eye.

"That," I said, suddenly sorry that I had said anything. "And other stuff."

I took Edna to my chest and sat there next to my wife.

"Naylor wanted me to help him. He thought I mighta heard somethin'."

When Regina put her hand on my knee I could have cheered.

"Why'd he think that?"

"I don't know. He knows that I used to get around pretty good. He just thought I might have heard somethin'. I told him that I couldn't help, but by then I needed a drink."

"Who was it?"

"Girl named Bonita Edwards."

Her hand moved to my shoulder.

"I still don't see why a policeman would come here to ask you about it. I mean, unless he thought you had something to do with it."

Regina always wanted to know why. Why did people call me for favors? Why did I feel I had to help certain people when they were in trouble? She never did know how I got her cousin out of jail.

"Well, you know," I said. "He probably thought that I was still in the street a lot. But I told him that I'm workin' for Mofass full-time now and that I don't get out too much."

I had lived a life of hiding before I met Regina. Nobody knew about me. They didn't know about my property. They didn't know about my relationship to the police. I felt safe in my secrets. I kept telling myself that Regina was my wife, my partner in life. I planned to tell her about what I'd done over the years. I planned to tell her that Mofass really worked for me and that I had plenty of money in bank accounts around town. But I had to get at it slowly, in my own time.

The money wasn't apparent in my way of living. So there was no need for her to be suspicious. I intended to tell her all about it someday. A day when I felt she could accept it, accept me for who I was.

"He knows that I get around the neighborhood is all, honey. They found that girl just twelve blocks from here."

"Could you help them?"

Edna stuck her hand down my shirt pocket and drooled on my chest.

"Uh-uh. I didn't know nuthin'. I told him that I'd ask around, though. You know it's an ugly thing."

Regina studied me like a pawnbroker looking for a flaw in a diamond ring. I bounced Edna in my arms until she started to laugh. Then I smiled at Regina. She just shook her head a little and studied me some more.

Edna felt like she weighed a hundred pounds and I laid her across my lap. I lay back myself.

Regina put her cool hand to my cheek. I could count each knuckle. I thought about that poor dead girl and the others.

Edna fell asleep. Regina took her to her crib. And I followed her to our bedroom. A room that was so small it was mostly bed.

She undressed and then moved to put on her nightclothes. But I embraced her before she got to her gown, my pants were down around my ankles. We fell back into the bed with her on top. She tried, weakly, to pull away but I held her and stroked her in the ways she liked. She gave in to my caresses but she wouldn't kiss me. I rolled up on top of her and held her head between my hands. She let my leg slip between hers but when I put my lips to hers she wouldn't open her mouth or her eyes. My tongue pushed at her teeth but that was as far as I got.

Regina let me hold her. She buried her face against my neck while I worked off my shorts and shirt. But when I moved to enter her she turned away from me. All of this was new. Regina wasn't as wild about sex as I was but she would usually come close to matching my ardor. Now it was like she wanted me but with nothing coming from her.

It excited me all the more, and even though I was dizzy with the alcohol in my blood, I cozied up behind her and entered her the way dogs do it.

"Stop, Easy!" she cried, but I knew she meant "Go on, do it!"

She writhed and I clamped my legs around hers. I bucked up against her and she grabbed the night table with such force that it was knocked over on to the floor. The lamp was pulled from the electric plug and the room went dark.

"Oh, God no!" she cried and she came, shouting and bucking and elbowing me hard.

When I relaxed my hold she pushed away and got up. I remember the light coming on and her standing there in the harsh electric glare. There was sweat on her face and glistening in her pubic hair. She looked at me with an emotion I could not read.

"I love you," I said.

I passed into sleep before her answer came.

It was afternoon in my dream. That golden sort of sunny day that they only get in southern California. Bonita Edwards was sitting under that tree with her legs out in front of her and her hands, palms up, at her side. There were birds, sparrows and jays, foraging through the grasses around her. A little breeze put the tiniest chill in the air.

"Who did this?" I asked the dead girl.

She turned to me. The bullet hole showed sky-blue in her head.

"What?" she asked in a timid little voice.

"Who did this to you?"

Then she started to cry. It was strange because it wasn't the sound that a woman makes when she cries.

Regina was leaning up against the tree with both hands. Her skirt was hiked up above her buttocks and a large naked man was taking her from behind. Her head whipped from side to side and she had a powerful orgasm but making the same kind of strange crying noises that Bonita Edwards made.

I hated them all. I could feel the hatred down in my body like a deep breath. I grabbed Bonita by the lapels of her pink party dress and lifted her. She hung down, heavy like the corpse she was, still crying.

Crying in that strange way. Like a kitten maybe. Or an inner tube squealing from a leak. Like a baby.

I opened my eyes, feeling chilly because I had kicked off the blankets. Edna was crying in little bursts. I got up and stumbled to the door. At the door I looked back to see that Regina had her eyes open. She was looking at the ceiling.

I was frightened by her. But I dismissed the fear as part of my dream.

Soon it will all be over, I thought. They'll catch the killer and my nightmares will go away.

SIX

I WENT TO THE kitchen to put Edna's formula on the stove. Then I got a diaper from the package that Jesus brought home every other day from LuEllen Stone.

Edna was crying in the corner of the living room where we'd set up her crib. I turned on the small lamp and loomed over her. That silenced the cries for a moment. Then I leaned over and kissed her on the cheek. That got a smile and a coo. I carried her back to the kitchen, where I laid her on a sheet rolled out over the kitchen table. I filled a red rubber tub with tepid water and undid the safety pin of her diapers.

She was crying again but not angrily. She was just telling me that she felt bad. I could have joined her.

I washed her with a soft chamois towel, saying little nonsense things and kissing her now and again. By the time she was clean all the tears were gone. The bottle was ready and I changed her fast. I held her to my chest again and gave her the bottle. She suckled and cooed and clawed at my nose.

I turned toward the door to see Regina there staring at us.

"You really love her, don't you, baby?" she asked.

I would rather her call me that sweet name than make love to any other woman in the world. It was like she opened a door, and I was ready to run in.

I smiled at her and in that moment I saw something shift in her eyes. It was as if a light went out, like the door closed before I got the chance to make it home.

"Baby," I said.

Edna shifted in my arms so that she could see her mother. She held one arm out to her and Regina took her from me.

"I need some money," Regina said.

"How much?"

"Six hundred dollars."

"I could do that." I nodded and sat down.

"How?"

I looked up at her, not really understanding the question.

"I asked you how, Easy."

"You asked if I could get you six hundred dollars."

When she shook her head her straightened hair flung from one side to the other and then froze there at the left side of her head.

"Uh-uh. I said that I needed that money. I ain't ax you fo'nuthin'. You coulda wanted t'know why I needed it. You coulda wanted to know how much I already have."

Out of the small back window, over the sink, the sky was turning from night to a pale whitish color. It felt like the world was getting larger and I wanted to run outside.

"Okay. All right. What you need it for?"

"I need clothes for me an' the baby, I got bills t'pay for my car, and my auntie down in Colette is sick and needs money t'go to the hospital."

"What's wrong with'er?"

"Stones. That's what the doctor said."

"An' how much you already got?" I almost felt like I was in charge.

"Uh-uh, Easy. I wanna know where you could get yo' hands on six hundred dollars," she snapped her fingers, "just like that."

"I don't ask you 'bout the money in yo' pocket, baby. That's your money," I said. "It ain't got nuthin' t'do with me."

"You don't need t'ask me nuthin', Easy Rawlins. You know I work right down at Temple. I get there at eight every mo'nin' an' I'm home at five-thirty every day. You know where my money come from."

"An' you know I work fo' Mofass," I argued. "I might not have reg'lar hours like you but I work just the same."

She snapped her fingers at me again. It made her furious that I could tell such a lie. "Ain't nobody clean an' sweep fo' a livin' could come up wit' that kinda money. You think I'm a fool?"

We had both come from hard times.

Regina was the eldest of fourteen Arkansas children. Her mother died giving birth to their last child. Her father disintegrated into a helpless drunk. Regina raised those children. She worked and farmed and smiled for the white store owners. I don't know the half of it but I do know that her life was hard.

She had once told me that she'd done things that she wasn't proud of to feed those hungry mouths.

"I ain't no criminal," I said. "That's all you gotta know. I could get your money if you need it. You want it?"

Edna, who was now cradled in her mother's arms, laughed loudly and threw her bottle to the floor. Her eyes and smile were bright and mischievous.

Regina bit her lip. That might have been a small concession

for some women but for her it was capitulation to a bitter foe.

"You should tell me what I wanna know, Easy."

"I ain't hidin' nuthin' from you, baby. You need money an' I could get it. That's because I love you an' Edna and I would do anything for you."

"Then why won't you tell me what I wanna know?"

I stood up fast and Regina flinched.

"I don't ask you about Arkansas, do I? I don't ask you what you had to do? When you tell me your auntie needs money I don't ask you why, at least I don't care. If you love me you just take me like I am. I ain't never hurt you, have I?"

Regina just stared.

"Have I?"

"No. You ain't laid a hand on me. Not that way."

"What's that s'posed to mean?"

"You don't hit me. It wouldn't matter if you did, though, 'cause I be out that door right after I shoot you if you ever laid a hand on me or my daughter." The defiance was back. It was better than her pain. "You don't hit me but you do other things just as bad."

"Like what?"

Regina was looking at my hands. I looked down myself to see clenched fists.

"Last night," she said. "What you call that?"

"Call what?"

"What you did to me. I didn't want none'a you. But you made me. You raped me."

"Rape?" I laughed. "Man cain't rape his own wife."

My laugh died when I saw the angry tears in Regina's eyes.

Edna stared at her mother wide-eyed, wondering who this new mother was.

"An' that ain't all, Easy. I wanted to name our daughter

Pontella after her great-grandmother. But you made us call her Edna. You said you just liked the name, but I know that you namin' her after that woman yo' crazy friend was married to."

She meant EttaMae.

She was right.

"All I wanna know," I said, "is if you want that six hundred dollars. I'm willin' t'get it but you gotta ask me."

Regina raised her beautiful black face and stared at me. She nodded after a while; it was a small, ungrateful gesture.

And an empty victory for me. I wanted her to be happy that I could help when she needed. But what she needed was something I couldn't give.

SEVEN

MADE MYSELF scarce for the next few evenings. I'd go out to different bars and drink until almost eleven and then come home. Everybody was in bed by then. I could breathe a little easier with no one to ask me questions.

Never, in my whole life, had anyone ever been able to demand to know about my private life. There was many a time that I'd give up teeth rather than answer a police interrogator. And here I was with Regina's silence and her distrust.

At night I dreamed of sinking ships and falling elevators.

It got so bad that on the third night I couldn't sleep at all

I could hear every sound in the house and the early traffic down Central Avenue. At six-thirty Regina got out of bed. A moment later Edna cried in the distance, then she laughed.

At seven the baby-sitter, Regina's cousin Gabby Lee came

over. She made loud noises that Edna liked and that always woke me up.

"Ooooo-ga wah!" the big woman cried. "Oooogy, ooogy, oogy, wah, wah, wah!"

Edna went wild with pleasured squeals.

At seven-fifteen the front door slammed. That was Regina going to her little Studebaker. I heard the tinny engine turn over and the sputter her car made as she drove off.

Gabby Lee was in the bathroom with Edna. For some reason she thought that babies had to be changed in the bathroom. I guess it was her idea of early toilet training.

When she came out I said, "Good morning."

Gabby Lee was a big woman. Not very fat really but barrel-shaped and a lighter shade than about half of the white people you're ever likely to meet. She had wiry strawberry hair and definite Negro features. She reserved her smile for other women and babies.

"You here today?" she asked me—the man who paid her salary.

"It's my house, ain't it?"

"Honeybell"—that was one of the nicknames she had for Regina—"wanted me to do some cleanin' today. You bein' here just be in my way."

"It is my house, ain't it?"

Gabby Lee harrumphed and snarled.

I went around her to relieve myself in the bathroom. There was a dirty diaper steaming in the sink.

The newspaper on the front porch was folded into a tube shape held by a tiny blue rubber band. I got it and started a pot of coffee in the old percolator that I bought three days after my discharge in 1945.

Jesus kissed me good morning. He had his book bag and wore

tennis shoes, jeans, and a tan short-sleeved shirt.

"You be good today and study hard," I said.

He nodded ferociously and grinned like a candidate for office. Then he ran out of the door and tore down out to the street.

He was never a great student. But since the fifth grade they put him in a special class. A class for kids with learning problems. His classmates ran a range from juvenile delinquent to mildly retarded. But his teacher, Keesha Jones, had taken a special interest in Jesus' reading. He sat up nearly every night with a book in his bed.

I poured myself a cup of coffee and settled down to the breakfast table intent on making some decision on what to do about Regina. Who knows, I might gotten somewhere if it wasn't for the headline of the *Los Angeles Examiner.*

WOMAN MURDERED
4TH VICTIM
KILLER
STALKS SOUTHLAND

Robin Garnett was last seen near a Thrifty's drugstore near Avalon. She was talking to a man who wore a trench coat with the collar turned up and a broad-rimmed Stetson hat. The article explained how she was later found in a small shack that sat on an abandoned lot four blocks away. She was beaten and possibly raped. She had been disfigured but the article didn't specify how. The article did explain why this murder was front-page news where the previous three were garbage liners—Robin Garnett was a white woman.

I found out that Robin was a coed at UCLA. She lived with her parents and had attended L.A. High. What the article didn't say was why she was down in that neighborhood in the first place.

I lit a Camel and drank my coffee. I opened the shades so that I could see them coming when they came.

At about nine, Gabby Lee emerged from my bedroom with Edna all dressed up for the park. I held out my arms and Edna screamed joyously. She reached for me but Gabby Lee held back.

"Bring my baby here to me," I said simply.

I held Edna and she held my nose. We made sounds at each other and laughed and laughed.

"We gotta go," Gabby Lee said after a while.

"I thought you was gonna clean?"

"I gotta be alone for that," she snapped. "Anyway it's a nice day out there and babies need some sun."

I handed my daughter back to the sour woman. Gabby lit up with Edna in her arms. That baby was so beautiful she could make a stone statue smile.

When they left the phone started ringing. It rang for a full minute before the caller disconnected. After that I took the phone off the hook.

I pulled a copy of Plato's writings from my shelf and read the "Phaedo" by the sunlight coming in my living-room window. My eyes hazed over when he died on that stone bench. I wondered at how it would be to be a white man; a man who felt that he belonged. I tried to imagine how it would feel to give up my life because I loved my homeland so much. Not the hero's death in the heat of battle but a criminal's death.

At eleven forty-seven a long black sedan parked in front of my house. Four men got out. Three of them were white men in business suits of various hues. The fourth was Quinten Naylor. They all got out of the car and looked around the neighborhood. They weren't timid about being deep in Watts. That's how I knew that they were all cops.

Quinten led the procession up to my door. They were all big men. The kind of white man who is successful because he towers over his peers. Almost every boss I had ever had was a white man and he was either a tall man or very fat; intimidation being the first requirement for obedience on the job.

I was at the door, behind a latched screen, when they mounted the porch.

"Good morning, Easy," Naylor said. He wasn't smiling. "We tried to call. I brought some men who want to discuss the news with you."

"I got to be somewhere in forty-five minutes," I said, not budging an inch.

"Open up, Rawlins." That came from a tight-lipped, Mediterranean-looking man in a two-piece silvery suit. I thought I recognized him but most cops blended into one brutal fist for me after a while.

"You got some paper for me to read?" I asked, not impolite.

"This is Captain Violette, Easy," Quinten said. "He's precinct captain."

"Oh," I mocked surprise. "An' these the other Pep Boys?"

Violette was my height, around six-one. The man next to him, behind Naylor, wore a threadbare baby-blue suit. He was an inch shorter and blunt in his appearance. His pasty white face was meaty and his ears were large. Black hairs sprouted everywhere on him. From his eyebrows, from his ears. He pushed his hand past Naylor to my door. It was blunt and hairy too.

"Hello, Mr. Rawlins. My name is Horace Voss. I'm a special liaison between the mayor's office and the police."

I could see that there was no turning this crowd away, so I unlatched the screen and shook Mr. Voss' hand.

"Well, come on in if you want, but I ain't even dressed yet, an' I gotta be somewhere soon."

Five big men made my living room seem like a small public toilet. But I got them all sitting somewhere. I leaned against the TV cabinet.

The man I hadn't met yet was the tallest one of all. He wore a tan wash-and-wear Sears suit. My uncle, Ogden Willy, owned one exactly like it in the Louisiana swamplands thirty years before.

He was thin and bony with long tapered fingers and deep green eyes. He was hatless and nearly bald with just a little black hair around his ears.

He crossed his long legs easily and smiled. He reminded me of a porcelain devil that was popular around that time in the Chinatown curio shops. "My name is Bergman, Mr. Rawlins. I work for the state—the governor. I'm not here in an official capacity. Just keeping an eye on these terrible events."

"Anybody want something to drink?" I asked.

"No," Violette said for everyone. But I think Mr. Voss would have liked to use his blunt fingers on a glass.

"We're here . . ." Quinten Naylor started to say but he was cut off by his superior, Violette.

"We're here to find out who's killing these girls," Violette said. He spoke with his upper lip tight against his teeth. "We don't want this crazy man running our streets."

"That's some shit," I said. "Excuse me, but I'ma have to go get me a beer if I gotta listen to this."

I went to the kitchen. Being independently employed I didn't have to worry about those officials getting me fired. I didn't have to worry about them beating me either. They were too important for that. Of course, they might have sent some goons later on. Maybe I should have been a little more deferential. But those men coming into my house turned my gut.

I filled the largest tumbler I had with ale and went back to the room. Voss looked at the foamy head, barely restraining himself from licking his lips.

"What the hell are you trying to do, Rawlins?" Violette yelled.

"Man, I'm in my own house, right? I ain't ask you over. Here you come crowdin' up my livin' room an' talkin' t'me like you got a blackjack in your pocket"—I was getting hot—"an' then you cryin' 'bout some dead girl an' I know they's been three before this one but you didn't give one good goddam! Because they was black girls an' this one is white!" If I had been on television every colored man and woman in America would have stood from their chairs and cheered.

Violette was up from his chair, but not to applaud. His face had turned bright red. That's when I remembered him. He was only a detective when he dragged Alvin Lewis out of his house on Sutter Place. Alvin had beaten a woman in an alley outside of a local bar and Violette had taken the call. The woman, Lola Jones, refused to press charges and Violette decided to take a little justice into his own hands. I remembered how red his face got while he beat Alvin with a police stick. I remembered how cowardly I felt while three other white policemen stood around with their hands on their pistols and grim satisfaction on their faces. It wasn't the satisfaction that a bad man had paid for his crime; those men were tickled to have power like that. A Nazi couldn't have done it better.

"Calm down, Anthony," the spectator Bergman ordered. "Mr. Rawlins, we're sorry to interrupt your day, but there is an emergency in the city. A man is killing women and we have to do something. I didn't know about this matter of the other women getting killed until today, but I promise you that we'll be looking into that. Still, no matter what way you look at it, we have a job to do."

"Police got a job to do. I'm just a citizen, a civilian. All I gotta do is cross on the green."

Mr. Bergman probably didn't even have a temper. He just smiled and nodded. "That's right, of course. It's Anthony's job to bring this man to justice. But you know that he could use some help, don't you, Mr. Rawlins?"

"I cain't help him. I'm not the police."

"But you can. You know all kinds of people in the community. You can go where the police can't go. You can ask questions of people who aren't willing to talk to the law. We need every hand we can get in on this, Mr. Rawlins." He held his hand out toward me but I left it alone.

"I'm in the middle of my own business, man. I cain't do nuthin'."

"Yes you can," Violette said in a guttural voice. I realized that I was wrong about men in that position. If Captain Violette had me alone I'd have been eating teeth about then.

"They already got a list of suspects, Easy," Quinten said.

"What do I care?" I answered him. "Go get 'em, put 'em in jail."

He mentioned a couple of names that I knew. But I told him that if he knew who did it there was no need to worry.

"We're also looking into Raymond Alexander," he said.

I felt every man in the room staring at me.

"You gotta be kiddin'," I said. Raymond Alexander, known to his friends as Mouse, was crazy and a killer, no doubt. He was also the closest thing I had to a best friend.

"No, Easy." Naylor was gritting his teeth. He was as mad as I was at those men. "Alexander frequents all the bars that the Negro women went to and he is known to go after white women."

"Him an' about thirty thousand other black men under the age of eighty."

"Do you think there's a flaw in the police approach, Mr. Rawlins?" Horace Voss asked.

"You just makin' up names, man. Mouse didn't kill no girls."

"Then who did?" Voss' blunt smile didn't seem quite human, it was more like the cross of a hungry bear and a happy man.

"How you expect me to know?"

"I expect it," Violette said. "Because if you don't you're going to find it very hard living down here among the blues."

A policeman with a sense of poetry.

"Is that a threat?"

Violette glared at me.

"Of course it isn't, Mr. Rawlins," Bergman said. "No one wants to threaten you. We all want the same thing here. There's a man killing women and he has to be brought to justice. That's what we all want."

Quinten was at the window peering out at the street. He knew that I had to go along with the program set out there before me. Captain Violette would run me to ground if I didn't. And Quinten was fuming because I refused to help when there were only black victims. Now that a white woman was dead I would agree to help. The air we breathed was racist.

"Lay off Raymond Alexander until I have time to nose around. He ain't killed no woman an' arrestin' him won't do nobody no good."

"If he's guilty, Rawlins, he'll fry like anybody else," Violette growled.

"I ain't tryin' to protect nobody, man," I said. "Just lemme look if that's what you want, an' sit on these arrests for a couple'a days."

Bergman stood up straight and tall. "That's it for me then. I'm sure the police and the mayor can give you all the help you need, Mr. Rawlins."

The other men rose.

Violette wouldn't even look at me, he just went to the door. Naylor looked but he didn't say anything. Bergman smiled and shook my hand warmly.

"Why are you down here, Mr. Bergman?" I asked.

"Just routine." His bottom lip jutted out an eighth of an inch. "Just routine."

Horace Voss took my hand in both of his.

"Call me at the Seventy-seventh," he said. "I'm there until this thing is over."

Then they were all gone from my house.

I hadn't hit the streets since my wedding. I tried to bury that part of my life. In one way, looking for this killer was like coming back from the dead for me.

EIGHT

I FRIED BLOOD sausages with onions and heated up a saucepan of red beans and rice for lunch. After I ate I mowed the lawn. It really didn't need it, but I wanted my new job to sink in and working in the garden calmed my nerves.

I couldn't seem to think of Bonita Edwards without seeing Regina crying. The dead woman's tragedy somehow resonated with Regina's anger.

I decided that I'd work out my problems with Regina after I'd seen to the job that L.A.'s representatives had given me.

But then I had to wonder at the strangeness of all those important white men thinking that they had to come all the way to my house in order to draft me.

I'd worked for city hall before but usually they called me downtown. They would have me wait on a cold marble bench while they preened and primped. Sometimes they'd call me to the police station and threaten me before asking my favors. But I'd never had a delegation at my house.

I expected Quinten Naylor, and maybe his white sidekick, but the people that had come were important. They were more important than one dead white girl. Women got killed all the time, and unless they were innocent mothers raped in their husbands' beds, the law didn't kick up such a big fuss.

Even though I'd eaten I had an empty feeling in the pit of my stomach. I filled the hole with three straight shots of bourbon. After that I felt calmer. Enough whiskey can take the edge off sunshine.

By one-thirty I was ready to go. I'd put on gray slacks and a gray square-cut shirt. My lapels were crimson, my shoes yellow suede. I had a light buzz on and my new Chrysler floated down the side streets like a yacht down some inland canals.

There was a small public library on Ninety-third and Hooper. Mrs. Stella Keaton was the librarian. We'd known each other for years. She was a white lady from Wisconsin. Her husband had a fatal heart attack in '34 and her two children died in a fire the year after that. Her only living relative had been an older brother who was stationed in San Diego with the navy for ten years. After his discharge he moved to L.A. When Mrs. Keaton had her tragedies he invited her to live with him. One year after that her brother, Horton, took ill, and after three months he died spitting up blood, in her arms.

All Mrs. Keaton had was the Ninety-third Street branch. She treated the people who came in there like her siblings and she treated the children like her own. If you were a regular at the library she'd bake you a cake on your birthday and save the books you loved under the front desk.

We were on a first-name basis, Stella and I, but I was unhappy that she held that job. I was unhappy because even though Stella was nice, she was still a white woman. A white woman from a place where there were only white Christians. To her Shakespeare was a god. I didn't mind that, but what did she know about the folk tales and riddles and stories colored folks had been telling for centuries? What did she know about the language we spoke?

I always heard her correcting children's speech. "Not 'I is,'" she'd say. "It's 'I am.'"

And, of course, she was right. It's just that little colored children listening to that proper white woman would never hear their own cadence in her words. They'd come to believe that they would have to abandon their own language and stories to become a part of her educated world. They would have to forfeit Waller for Mozart and Remus for Puck. They would enter a world where only white people spoke. And no matter how articulate Dickens and Voltaire were, those children wouldn't have their own examples in the house of learning—the library.

I had argued with Stella about these things before. She was sensitive about them but when you told her that some man standing on a street corner telling bawdy tales was something like Chaucer she'd crinkle her nose and shake her head. She was always respectful, though. They often take the kindest white people to colonize the colored community. But as kind as Mrs. Keaton was, she reflected an alien view to our people.

"Good morning, Ezekiel," Mrs. Keaton said.

"Stella."

"How is that little Jesus?"

"He's fine, just fine."

"You know, he's in here every Saturday. He always wants to

help more than he reads, but I think he's getting somewhere. Sometimes I come up on him and it seems as if he's mouthing the words and reading to himself."

There was nothing wrong with the boy's larynx, the doctors had told me that. He could have talked if he wanted to.

"Maybe he'll get around to it one day," I said, more finishing the thought in my head than talking to her.

She smiled with perfect little pearls along her pink gums. Mrs. Keaton was small and wiry. She had the same color hair as Gabby Lee. But Mrs. Keaton's color came out of a bottle, whereas Gabby's had come from the genetic war white men have waged on black women for centuries.

"You got the newspapers for the last two months, Stella?"

"Sure do. *Times* and *Examiner.*"

She took me into a back room that had a long oak reading table. The room smelled of old newspaper. Along all the shelves were stacks of the papers I wanted.

The papers pretty much said what Naylor told me. The articles were buried in the back pages and there was no connection made between the crimes.

Willa Scott's and Juliette LeRoi's whereabouts on the nights of their deaths were unknown. Their occupations were listed as waitress. Willa though, it seemed, was unemployed.

Bonita Edwards was in a bar the night she died. She'd had quite a few drinks and had been seen with quite a few men. But, witnesses said, she left alone. Of course, that didn't mean anything—she could have made a date with some man who was married and didn't want it to get around what he was doing. She could have made a date with a murderer who had the same reasons for not being seen.

I put that information together with what I'd already read, and heard, about Robin Garnett.

Robin Garnett didn't make any sense at all. She lived with

her parents on Hauser, way over in the western part of L.A. Her father was a prosecuting attorney for the city and her mother stayed home. Robin was a coed at UCLA. She was twenty-one and still a sophomore. She'd just recently returned from a trip to Europe, the paper said, and was expecting to major in education.

She was a pretty girl. (Robin was the only victim to have a photograph printed.) She had sandy hair and a very nice, what old folks call a healthy, smile. Her hair was pulled back, very conservative. Her blouse was of the button-down-the-front variety, and every button was buttoned. The photo was for her parents, for a yearbook, it didn't give the slightest hint of what she might have really been like.

It certainly didn't say why she was the fourth of a series of murders that started out with three black women. Even if a white woman somehow fit into this scheme of murders, why would somebody kill three good-time girls and then go after a bobby-soxer?

I went out to the main room perplexed.

"Did you find what you were looking for, Ezekiel?"

"Naw." I shook my head. "I mean, yeah . . ." She frowned when I said that. I knew she wanted to correct me with "Yes."

John McKenzie's bar had grown over the years. He'd added a kitchen and eight plush booths for dinner. He even hired a short-order cook to burn steaks and boil vegetables. There was a stage for blues and jazz performances. And waitresses, three of them, serving the bar and the round tables that surrounded the stage.

John still owned Targets but Odell Jones' name was on the deeds. John had had too much trouble with the law to get a liquor license, so he needed a front man. Odell was ideal. He was a mild-mannered man, semiretired, two years shy of sixty, and twenty-two years older than I.

Odell was sitting in his regular booth toward the back. He was sipping at a beer and reading the *Sentinel*—L.A.'s largest Negro publication. We hadn't exchanged words in over three years and it still broke my heart that I had lost such a good friend. But when you're a poor man struggling in this world you rub up against people pretty hard sometimes. And the people you hurt the most are poor sons just like yourself.

Once I was deep in trouble and I asked Odell to lend me a hand. How was I to know that his minister would end up dead? How could I blame him for hating me either?

"Easy," John greeted me. His dark face was stony and expressionless.

"John. Gimme a fist of little Johnnie Walker." That meant four fingers.

While he poured I asked him, "You hear anything about them girls gettin' killed?"

"I knowed all them girls, Easy. Every one."

I thought again of Bonita Edwards. I slugged back half of my drink.

"All of 'em?"

John looked me in the eye and nodded.

"Even Robin Garnett?"

"I don't know nuthin' 'bout no Robin what-have-ya but I know that white girl got her picture in the paper. That was Cyndi Starr an' they ain't no lyin' 'bout that." He looked at a stool next to me. Maybe a stool she'd once sat in. "Yeah, Cyndi—the White Butterfly."

"The what?"

"That was her stage name. She was a damned stripper, man."

"And you say her name was Cyndi Starr?"

"That was her name, least that's what they called her. You know, she was just like all these other girls. It's only these white people makin' all that fuss. They coulda been sayin' somethin' 'fore she got killed."

"You sure, John? Paper says she went to college in West L.A. They said she lived with her parents out there."

"I read it. But just 'cause you read it in the paper don't make it true. If she went t' college she studied takin' off her clothes fo'men to watch'er, an' if she lived wit'er parents they lived right down here on Hollywood Row."

"You mean she lived down here?"

"Uh-huh, right down on the Hollywood Row. An' that ain't all I know either."

"Yeah?"

"That other one, that Juliette LeRoi, she was down at Aretha's right around the night she got killed."

"How do you know?"

"I know 'cause she got into a fight wit' some boy or sumpin'. Coy Baxter told me that the boy was so messed up that he had to go to the emergency room at Temple."

"Aretha's, you say?"

John nodded again.

I asked him a few other questions and he answered them as well as he could.

My car started up with a roar. I hit the gas and felt the tug of gravity as she pulled toward the corner. I turned the steering wheel and felt the swing of the back end as I straightened out for the main drag.

That's when I saw the woman. She was jaywalking and pushing a baby carriage.

I hit the brakes and felt the back end fishtail. I got a panorama of the shops and stores on the east side of the street. The car turned completely around. By the time I was facing the young mother again, she was yelling, "Motherfucker! Motherfucker! Who in hell! Fuck you!" and things like that.

Another car behind me hit his brakes. The squeal seemed to go on forever, but it didn't hit anything. The woman stopped screaming and gathered her baby up in her arms. She ran for the sidewalk, leaving the carriage in the middle of the street.

My heart was beating fast. The woman was trying to calm down the hollering baby.

I started my engine back up and drove off thinking about how my life had gone out of control.

NINE

BONE STREET WAS local history. A crooked spine down the center of Watts' jazz heyday, it was four long and jagged blocks. West of Central Avenue and north of 103rd Street, Bone Street was broken and desolate to look at by day, with its two-story tenementlike apartment buildings and its mangy hotels. But by night Bones, as it was called, was a center for late-night blues, and whiskey so strong that it could grow hairs on the glass it was served in. When a man said he was going to get down to the bare Bones he meant he was going to lose himself in the music and the booze and the women down there.

The women, in the late forties and even into the early fifties, were all beautiful; young and old, in satins, silks, and furs. They came in the back-room clubs fine and sassy, and daring any man to wipe the snarl from their lips. They'd come in and listen to

Coltrane, Monk, Holiday, and all the rest, drinking shot for shot with their men.

It was a bold and flashy time. But by that evening all the shine had rubbed off to expose the base metal below. The sidewalks were broken, sporting hardy weeds in their cracks. Some clubs were still there but they were quieter now. The jazzmen had found new arenas. Many had gone to Paris and New York. The blues was still with us. The blues would always be with us. The blues will always be with us.

Sonny Terry, Brownie McGee, Lightnin' Hopkins, Soup-spoon Wise, and a hundred others passed through the hotels and back-street dives that still cluttered Bone. In the old days the jazzmen came in fancy cars like Cadillacs. The bluesmen came by Greyhound, sometimes by thumb.

The women were still there. But their clothes didn't fit right anymore. Their eyes were more hungry than wild. All the promise after the war had drained away and a new generation was asking, "Where's ours?"

Rock and roll waged a war over the radio and in the large dance clubs. Bone Street was forgotten except by those lost souls who wanted a taste of the glitter of their day.

Aretha's was in an alley halfway down the 1600 block of Bone. It had other names over the years, and different addresses too. It was a legal bar, more or less. But the waitresses were all scantily clad girls and the police found it proper to shut Charlene Mars down every once in a while. Charlene ran Aretha's, or whatever it was called at the time. Over the years it had been named the Del-Mar, the Nines, Swing, and Juanita's. The name and the address changed but it was always the same club. The girls had different names too and even different faces, but they did the same work.

That year they wore a very short black skirt over a one-piece brown bathing suit and black fishnet stockings. The room was long and narrow with a very high ceiling and a stage at the far end. Down the left side of the room ran an oak bar tended by Westley.

Westley and Charlene had started as lovers. She was skinny and he wore fine clothes. They both loved jazz and, along with John from Targets, had the best hornmen and vocalists in the country. But a lot of whiskey and fine men, and fine women, moved through their lives. Charlene bought a small house in Compton, where she took care of her retarded brother. Westley, a tall large-handed man, took to sleeping in the bar.

The whites of his eyes were yellow and he stooped over. His arms were as strong as iron cables.

He looked at me and nodded at an empty table, but I walked up to the bar.

"Hey, West."

"Easy."

"Johnnie Walker," I said.

He turned away to grant my request.

The room was dark. The phonograph played a light and lively version of "Lady Blue." With no introduction a buxom woman, well into her fifties, jiggled out onstage. She wasn't wearing much and all of that was a shiny banana yellow against high-brown skin. She carried a long yellow plume, which she waved along with her breasts and thighs.

There were eight small tables opposite the bar and a cluster of them before the stage. Black men and women sat here and there. Fragile ribbons of smoke rose from gaudy aluminum ashtrays. A waitress moved petulantly from table to table. "You want sumpin' else t'drink?" was the question I heard her ask most often. The answer was almost always "No."

This was the early crowd, not huge tippers. They were kind of a warm-up act for the customers, mostly men, who came later.

Charlene sat right up next to the stage, sipping at a lime-colored drink. She had always claimed that the girls never did anything that they didn't want to do, but I'd known women who'd been fired from there because a customer had complained that they were "unfriendly."

I took the whiskey and moved toward the stage. Closer up you could see the makeup that the banana dancer wore. Her face looked like a carved wooden mask.

"Easy Rawlins!" Charlene squealed.

I took her hands and kissed her moist face.

"Charlene."

In a fit of improvisation the banana dancer moved downstage and brushed the back of my neck with her plume.

"Sit'own, baby." Charlene pulled an empty chair away from a table where an old man had his head resting on his hands.

"Kinda slow, huh?" I asked.

She pawed at me with a pudgy red-fingered hand. "It's early, Easy. Fern just do her li'l thing out there to get the stage ready for the young girls tonight."

I smiled and finished my drink. Before ordering another one I lit a Camel and inhaled deeply.

I didn't have a plan. I wasn't a policeman. I didn't have a notepad. Maybe we'd talk about the night that Juliette LeRoi was murdered. Maybe not.

"Could I get you somethin', mister?" the waitress asked. She was a high-yellow woman with straightened hair that came down and curled around her ears, like black modeling clay. She had light brown skin and freckles. Her large lips were in a permanent pout. She stood very close to me.

"Ask Westley what he had, Elaine, an' bring that," Charlene said for me. Then she said, "I thought you was married, Easy Rawlins."

I was watching Elaine move toward the bar.

"What would you do if you got married, Charlene?" I asked.

"Same things I do now, I guess."

"I mean, you got all this property an' stuff. What would you do if your husband didn't have all what you have?"

Charlene had big round cheeks that crowded her eyes when she smiled. "We'd have to sign us some papers before we got together. You know a po' niggah get next to that much money an' he's liable to go crazy. You know he'd be just like you."

"What you mean?" As I spoke Elaine returned and put the glass down in front of me.

Charlene took the waitress by the wrist and pulled her so close that the young woman was almost on her lap. She turned Elaine toward me so that I could get a good look at her. Elaine looked down at her breasts and smiled. Her long fake lashes enchanted me. I didn't know whether to take a drag off of my cigarette or a sip from my glass.

"Just like you, Easy. Here you are lookin' at Elaine. Now just think if you saw my deeds an' my cash register an' then this here girl's titties an' legs . . ."

I couldn't take my eyes off what Charlene was talking about. Elaine looked up at me. She was smiling but her eyes were cold.

I actually felt myself beginning to sweat.

Charlene slapped the girl on the butt and pushed her toward the bar. Elaine brushed me with one of those thighs as she went by. She even put a hand on my shoulder before walking away.

"Man got nuthin' cain't never get enough, Easy."

"What about a woman?" I asked. My throat was tight.

"What you worried 'bout?" Charlene smiled a warm, friendly smile. "You don't make enough to have no problem like that."

"I got a house," I said. "I got a car and a job that pays me a paycheck. That's enough fo' some women, ain't it?"

"I guess." She nodded. "Some women will take the dirty underwear right out of the hamper before they go. But unless you got sumpin' worth takin', Easy, I wouldn't be worried 'bout it. An' if you is worried, maybe you should cut it off now. That why you here?"

"Say what?"

"You wanna start playin' 'round?" Charlene's business wasn't a subtle one. " 'Cause you know Elaine likes you."

"Naw." I shook my head and smiled. "I just wanted to ask you that question, that's all."

"Okay. But if you need anything, you know where t'come to. Gettin' people together is my business."

"Business good?" I asked.

Charlene nodded. She was watching two men come in. Westley was watching too. He could pour and look at the same time.

" 'Cause I thought things mighta gotten kinda hard for you."

"Why?"

"After that thing with Julie LeRoi."

"What you mean?"

"Hey!" I put my hands in the air. "It's just that people been talkin' 'bout how she was here the night she was killed an' how the man that killed her was probably here, an' then he killed all them other girls."

"Caintnobodyprovethat," she said in machine-gun talk.

"Hey, like I said, it's just what I heard."

"Listen." She held a fat finger up to my face. "That Julie LeRoi was a tramp. She come here tryin' t'get her rent money. Now you know she be in five places in any night an' out on the corner if that don't work."

"But I heard she was here with a boyfriend." I snapped my fingers trying to remember something I didn't know.

"That boy Gregory?" she exploded. "He was her john. It's

just that another one wanted her too an' he had more muscles, that's all."

I nodded, sipped.

"I see," I said, very seriously. "Anyway, it's cool now, right? Nobody's scared."

"Don't let 'em fool ya," Charlene said and pointed down the long room. "They all scared. Scared t'death. But what could they do? Poor woman all alone needs men fo'sumpin'. Maybe it's that night's rent an' maybe more, but she need sumpin'. An' these men is hungry too. Hungry fo'drink an' hungry fo'love."

I let her wisdom settle for a moment, then I said, "Well, I better be goin'."

When I stood up I felt the room bob a little as if I were on a ship.

"See ya," I said.

"Bye, Easy." Charlene smiled. "You take care now, baby."

I paid Westley on the way out. At the bar I tapped Elaine's shoulder and gave her a rolled-up dollar bill. When she smiled in the stronger light of the bar I noticed that she was missing one of her lower front teeth. That one simple, human fact excited me more than all of Charlene's bold talk.

When I staggered out of the door it wasn't only the whiskey that had me drunk.

THE BARS AND clubs on and around Bone Street were many. I wouldn't have been able to hit all of them in one night, but I didn't have to, because I was looking for a special kind of joint. A place like Charlene's that catered to love-starved and sex-starved men, and sometimes women. A place that offered a little more than whiskey and blues. There were just a handful of clubs that fit those needs.

There was the Can-Can, run by Caleb Varley. At one time Caleb had a regular revue. But he had to cut back to a piano player and two sisters, Wanda and Sheila Rollet, who danced around artistically in golden glitter and glue. Then there was Pussy's Den, a pickup bar where B-girls had a couple of drinks before heading for an apartment, an alley, or an hourly motel.

DeCatur's still had Dixieland musicians.

The Yellow Dog and Mike's were one step down on the evolutionary scale. These were bars where the criminal element hung out. Gangsters and gamblers. Men who had done hard time for every crime you could think of. But there was a place for them, there were women for them too. Mostly your larger women. The kind who could take the punishment; either physical or grief. Both of these bars had back rooms where doctors sometimes came to patch a gunshot or knife wound. Where lawyers met clients that couldn't be seen going into an office in the daylight. And where women got on their knees for five minutes and five dollars, for a man who might not have seen a woman in five years.

I had been out of the bar scene since I got married, so most people were happy to see me. They were happy to talk. But nobody knew a thing.

I saw a fight in DeCatur's. A young boy named Jasper Filagret decided to take his woman, Dorthea, off the streets. He came in blustering and he went out bleeding. Dorthea left ten minutes later with another man. She had her fingers in his pocket while he rubbed the knuckles of his right hand.

I ran into an old acquaintance at the Yellow Dog. Roger Vaughn was his name. Roger was only five-six, but he had the shoulders of a heavyweight. He'd been drunk in a bar on Myrtle Street some years before. He'd wanted another drink but the bartender wanted to go home to his wife. He told Roger that he had to go and Roger said, "After one more drink." That's when the six-foot barman made his mistake. He grabbed Roger and Roger socked him, twice. The bartender was dead before he hit the floor. Roger did seven straight years for manslaughter. If the bartender had been a black man Roger wouldn't have done half that.

"Easy," Roger Vaughn said. He was hunched over his table with his big hands around a tumbler full of beer.

"Roger. You out at last, huh, man?"

"Not fo'long," he said, nodding in a way that made him seem wise.

"You paid your time, man. They cain't take you back unless you want 'em to." I pulled a chair up to his lonely table.

"Motherfucker took my money."

Roger was drunk and loose in the tongue. I knew that if I let him talk he would help me all he could. But I might have to hear things I didn't want to hear to get there. I was half drunk myself, otherwise I'd have bowed out right then.

"Motherfucker been doin' my wife. Right there in my own house. She come up to Soledad an' be smilin' at me. But all the time she comin' home to him. She comin' home t'him."

The glass broke in Roger's grip; more like it just crumbled. Beer, mixed with a little blood, ran over the table. I threw some paper napkins from the dispenser on the spill and handed Roger my handkerchief. He looked at me with a depth of gratitude.

"Thank you, Easy. You're a friend, man. A real friend."

You could buy a drunk's friendship with a handful of feathers and a sprinkle of salt.

"Thanks, Roger," I said. I patted his rocky shoulder across the table. "I was tryin' t'find somethin' out."

"What's that?"

"You knew Bonita Edwards?"

"Uh-huh, yeah, I knew'er. You know that was a shame what happened that girl."

Blood soaked more and more into my rag.

"Hold that thing tight, Roger. You bleedin' pretty good there."

He gazed down at his hand and seemed surprised to see the bloody cloth. Then he clenched the hand into a fist and the whole thing disappeared.

"What you wanna know 'bout Bonnie?"

"She was a friend'a mines, Roger, so I'm askin' if anybody seen'er 'round 'fore she got killed."

He shook his head slowly, his eyes moved loosely as he did. "Nope," he said. "An' you know if I did I'da kilt him jus' like I'ma kill . . ."

"Did you know what she was doin' that last week?" I asked, partly because I wanted to know and partly to distract him.

"I don't wanna cause you no pain, Easy, but I think she was down on Bethune."

I tried to look like I was bothered by this information. When somebody said Bethune they meant a whorehouse run by a white man named Max Howard and his wife, Estelle.

"Thank you, Roger," I said, as seriously as I could.

"Woman tear your heart out, man." Roger shook his head again. "An' that's what I'ma do to Charles Warren. He got my kids callin' him Daddy. He got my wife callin' him Daddy too. She be fuckin' me like it's all that love an' stuff. But she goin' t'see him Friday. I seen it on a note in her purse."

It was time for me to go. I should have gone. But instead I said, "Man, you don't know what it is."

Roger's head moved slowly as he turned his face upward to look at me. The rest of his body was rock-solid and tense.

He said, "What?"

"All I'm sayin' is give'er a chance, man. Maybe it ain't what you think. I mean, she did come up to Soledad to see ya, right?"

Roger just stared.

"Woman wanna leave a man don't come up t'see him but the first few months," I continued. "But yo' wife come up the whole time, right?"

He wouldn't nod. We weren't friends anymore.

"Think about it, Roger. Talk to her."

I got up and backed away from the table. Roger followed me

with his eyes. I decided to let him keep the handkerchief. Maybe when he looked at the bloody rag he'd remember what I said and refrain from killing Charles Warren.

The Howards' house was a big yellow thing. It had been a plain, single-story house at one time but they kept adding to it. First they made the garage into their living quarters so that the rest of the house could be used for business. Then they added a room on the other side. A second floor was put on in 1952 with a flat roof supporting a flower garden that Estelle tended. At some point they bought the house next door and annexed it by building a long hall-like structure across the yard. The original house was wood but the new addition was brick. The city started giving them zoning problems in '55 so they farmed out the girls for a while and had the whole thing painted yellow so that it would at least look of a piece.

I guess the city agent backed off or, more likely, was paid off. The girls came back, and along with them their regular customers. Nobody complained. Max, Estelle, and twelve women lived there—raising families, working hard, and going to church on Sundays.

I was drunk. The only reason I didn't have an accident driving the eight blocks to Bethune was that I didn't think about driving and somehow steered from instinct. I pushed the button in the center of the lion's mouth at the front door but I didn't feel my finger. I didn't hear the bell either, but, as I said, it was a big house.

A mule-faced woman answered the door. She was more than forty and less than sixty-five but that was all I could say about her age. Her platinum-blond hair cascaded to her shoulders like Marlene Dietrich's. Her skin was black. Her face had many folds in it. And her eyes were the color and sheen of wet mud. Her small hands, which she held before her pink bathrobe, looked as if they could crush stones.

"Estelle," I said. I had a stupid grin on my face. I could see it in the bronze-framed mirror that dominated the wall at Estelle's back. She peered at me as if I might have been a dream that would disappear.

I grinned on.

"What you want?" she asked, not in a friendly way at all.

"Thought I might have a drink an' some company." I shuddered. "It's cold out tonight."

"You already had enough t'drink, an' you got a wife t'keep you warm."

"Business so good you turnin' it away?"

Estelle pushed at a loose lock of her wig and the whole thing turned askew on her head. She didn't seem to notice, though.

"Ain't nuthin' that good. I just don't trust you, Easy. I hear all kindsa things 'bout you. What you want? I ain't axin' no mo'."

I tried to make the grin a little more sincere by looking into my own eyes in the mirror.

"Like I said. I want a drink an' some soft friendship. That's all."

"Why come here?"

"I been told that that girl . . ." I snapped my fingers again, looking for something I didn't know again. "You know, that li'l one, Bonita Edwards' friend."

The mud in Estelle's eye hardened to stone. "Nita Edwards is dead."

"I ain't lookin' 'ther, it's just that I cain't remember her li'l friend's name."

"You mean Marla?" The look on Estelle Howard's mug would have deterred a rhinoceros.

"I don't know." I held up my hands. The smile muscles in my cheeks ached. "Jackson Blue told me 'bout her, but all he remembered was that she was Bonita's friend."

I smiled and she scowled for another thirty seconds or so, then she said, "You better com'on in fo' you let all the heat out."

ELEVEN

WE WENT DOWN a long hall that was papered with yellow and orange velvet. There were small dark-stained tables every few feet with clean ashtrays and dishes of hard candy on them. This led to a largish room that had blue sofas along each cream wall. There were lamps here and there, all of them turned on. A woman and a boychild sat on a sofa before wall-length maroon drapes. She was Mexican with a lot of cleavage and makeup, backed by a mane of luxurious black hair. He was black and scrawny but had the largest brown eyes I'd ever seen—his mother's eyes.

"Wait here," Estelle said, batting at her wig.

She exited out a door on the opposite side of the room.

"Hey, mister?"

She was looking at me, smiling. The boy had something that came close to hatred in his beautiful eyes.

"Yeah?"

"Is it 'Peter and me went' or 'Peter and I went'?" She curled her lip and flared her nostril on the last sentence. I noticed that the boy had a straight-backed pad of paper on his lap.

" 'Peter and I,' like, 'Peter and I went to the store.' You see, you know because if you cut it down and said 'I went to the store' it would be better than 'Me went to the store.' "

The mother looked leery. The boy wanted to tear my heart out.

"You live here?" I asked.

"Yes." Her smile dazzled. She wasn't beautiful but she projected warmth.

"Hey, Pedro!"

The boy stopped scowling at me long enough to peer at the old white man coming through the door.

"Come here, boy!"

I was surprised that such an old and feeble-looking man could produce such volume.

He was tall and stooped over like Westley, but even more. He could almost look little Pedro in the eye. Max Howard fished a coin out of his pocket and flipped it at the boy. Pedro caught it and checked to see what it was—he didn't look disappointed.

Max had a full head of long white hair. During that time only old men could get away with that kind of hairstyle. He kept his head up, reminding me of a vulture scanning the horizon for the spectacle of death. He wore an old-fashioned three-button black suit with a starched white shirt and a silken blue-and-black tie. His shoes were older than I was but they were in perfect repair.

"Mr. Howard," I said.

"Rawlins, isn't it?"

"Yes, sir. Easy Rawlins." I didn't hold out my hand and he kept his claws in his pockets.

Max pressed his lips out and swiveled his head toward the mother and child. He might have nodded, maybe he silently mouthed something, but Pedro's mother gathered the boy up and hurried out of the room.

"Have a seat, Easy," Max Howard said.

I sat and he stood before me. His skin was like bleached onion parchment, crinkled and ghastly white.

He blinked. I crossed my legs. Somewhere far away a motor cruised down the street.

"What do you want here, Easy?" The question was straightforward.

"A woman," I said in kind.

His smiling lips quivered like a pair of light blue earthworms. "I don't think so," he said.

He blinked again. I uncrossed my legs.

After what seemed like a long time he said, "Twenty dollars."

I took out the bill and handed it over. He brought it right up to his face and squinted. Then he nodded and went back the way he'd come.

A few minutes later a short woman wearing a checkered muumuu that barely came down to her legs walked in. She had big red lips and round thighs. Her hair was permed into big floppy curls. Her eyes were big and round and ready to look into mine.

"Com'on," she said. Then she turned and walked away.

I followed her up the stairs. Her dress didn't hide a thing.

We went down a hallway that looked like it belonged in a hotel. There were doors on each side with numbers on them. She opened door seven and ushered me in.

"How you wan'it?" she asked my back.

When I turned around she'd taken off the dress.

"Just a little talk." I don't think I stuttered, but the girl smiled as if I had.

"What you wanna talk about?" One of her upper front teeth was solid gold. There was a nipple-sized mole just above her left nipple.

"You Marla?"

"Com'on." She pointed at the bed. "Sit'own."

We sat side by side with her thigh against my pant leg.

"You Marla?" I asked again.

"Uh-huh."

"I wanna know about Bonita Edwards."

"She dead."

Marla took my hand in hers and rubbed the knuckles against her nipple. It hardened and became very long.

Marla smiled. "She like you."

"I wanna know about Bonita Edwards."

"What you wanna know?"

"Did somebody want her dead? Anybody you know?"

Marla sat back with her hands propping her body from behind. "You workin' for the cops? 'Cause the cops already came here an' we told'em that we didn't know nuthin'. Bonita had the day off an' she just never came back."

"I just wanna find out what happened to her, That's all."

"Max an' Estelle say I better watch out about you. They say you bad news an' I jus' better fuck you an' keep my mouf shut."

"S'pose I want you to use yo' mouf on me?"

Marla laughed and grabbed my arm. It was a very good laugh, lots of feeling behind it.

"That was a good one." She smiled at me and I realized that I was sitting on the bed with a naked young woman.

Then came three raps at the door. "Five minutes!" a man's voice said. It wasn't Max Howard.

"You got forty mo' dollars, mister?" Marla asked.

"How come?"

"They only give ya ten minutes for' twenty an' they knock

after five, you know, to hurry up. But if you pay again they let you go forty-five minutes fo' just sixty bucks."

I gave her the money.

She ran out in the hall without putting on a stitch.

In the room alone I considered going out of the window. Maybe she'd tell them what I asked her and they'd come back with a gun. I hadn't come armed. The whiskey was wearing off and I wasn't so brave anymore. I wasn't so sure.

The door opened and Marla came back with a bottle of scotch, two glasses, and her natural charm.

She was grinning. "We got almost a hour an' this bottle. You wan'it?"

She poured the two glasses full and settled on the bed beside me, her legs open wide enough to expose a thick mat of pubic hair. "So what you wanna know?"

"Same thing. A guy wants me t'find out about Bonita. He's upset about what happened and maybe he'd like t'say sumpin' to the guy that did it."

"What guy?"

"That ain't none'a yo' business, honey." I took a long drink and poured another glass full. Marla did the same and laughed.

"Bonita didn't have no boyfriend," she said speculatively. "She didn't even like men, not like me. An' I cain't think'a no-body wanna do that."

I sloshed back another drink. "Had to be somebody. Nobody kills you fo'nuthin'."

"Baby, you ain't never been in this business if you think that." Marla leaned forward to shake her head, and I realized that her curls were a wig.

"How old are you?" I demanded.

"Nineteen. An' I seen girls killed before. I seen men come at'em with a baseball bat and a razor blade. I seen men come up these here steps with a dog they want the girl t'get friendly wit'. Uh-huh. I might just be a girl but I'm a woman too. I been a woman since I was eleven."

We both drank some more. Marla put her hand way up on my thigh.

"Who wanna know 'bout Bonita?" she asked.

"I can't say. They payin' me an' I ain't s'posed t'tell."

"You wanna fuck me?"

"Did Bonita know them other girls got killed?" I took another drink.

"Uh-uh."

"How do you know?"

"She told me. I know'd Julie LeRoi myself an' when I told Nita 'bout her she said, 'Who?' " Marla laughed. " 'Who?' Just like a owl."

I don't know how we started kissing, but there I was on my back and Marla was on top of me. I was so drunk I could barely feel our lips or tongues but something stronger than feeling was driving me.

When she was pulling down my pants I said, "How 'bout the other ones, Willa Scott or a stripper named Cyndi Starr?"

"You want me t'suck this thing or talk?"

I didn't say anything and she didn't either.

A long time later the knocks came on the door again.

"You gotta get dressed," Marla said.

I put on my pants and she slipped on her shift.

I got my money's worth. Bonita Edwards was from Dallas and had only been in L.A. three months. She came right to Max and Estelle's. She had an apartment but hardly ever went there. She didn't know Willa Scott, but Marla wasn't sure about Cyndi Starr.

"Marla?"

"What?"

"You ever do any work outside of here? I mean, does anybody ever hire you to meet'em on you' day off or sumpin'?"

"Sometimes."

I knew from her smile that she'd hate me.

"Did Bonita?"

"That what you wanna know?" she snapped. "Why'ont you go on down to the mortuary an' jump on her?"

"Com'on, Marla. This is how I get paid."

"I don't know."

"You don't know what?"

"I don't know nuthin'!" she yelled, putting her fists up to her ears. Then she jumped up and ran out of the door.

I took a moment to grab my shirt before going after her.

When I made it to the hallway a snakish white man was standing where Marla was supposed to be. He wore a tapered green suit that was large in the shoulders and thin at the hips. The suit matched his eyes. He smiled the way a snake would smile if serpents had lips.

"Hold on there, son," he hissed. "Playtime is over."

I was drunk, but not so drunk I didn't know that my reflexes were shot. I became as quiet as I could be, gathering all of my strength for one move.

"Why you after Marla?" Snake-lips was almost polite.

He raised his eyes a little, glancing over my right shoulder.

I heard the man behind me grunt. That was enough warning for me to avoid the blackjack aimed at my head. I moved to the right long enough to see a squat Negro stumble behind the force of his thrust. I let him fall and I threw a punch that landed on the side of Snake-lips' jaw. He fell back against the wall.

Little men are, on the whole, more agile than larger ones. The little Negro was already on his feet and swinging his sap. I moved enough not to take the full brunt of the blow but it did graze my head above the left ear.

The impact felt much like when a large vehicle, a bus for example, hits its brakes and sends you reeling. Then came the colors: red amoebae cut by yellow shards and peppered with black holes.

I aimed my fist for the place that I had last seen the little man's face. I felt a meaty impact.

Then I was stumbling down the stairs. I ran into a woman wearing a black negligee in the room where the Mexican woman and her child had been learning to read.

"Oh!" she exclaimed with a laugh in her voice. But when she looked at my face she backed away. I reached out to her after we'd collided; as she pulled away the material of her gown felt rough against my palms.

My bare feet were cold on the pavement outside. Marla's strong perfume and her female scent permeated my clothes. Maybe she liked me? I laughed and hurt and almost threw up. I shouldn't go home smelling like I did but I had to go home.

It took a long time for me to read the time off my copper-faced Gruen "very thin" watch. By then it was two forty-five. I took a deep breath and started the engine.

I drove very slowly down to my street, parking far enough away that Regina wouldn't be awakened by the familiar sound of my motor. I spent a whole minute opening the gate so it wouldn't squeak. Then I went in through Jesus' side door.

Jesus lay on his back with his mouth open. He would have slept through an earthquake. I took off my clothes and shoved them under his bed.

I sat in the bathtub letting the water trickle in slowly. Marla's smell was down my legs and under my fingernails. It was in my hair and on my breath.

After a long time I came out of the tub. I put on a robe and went to the baby's crib. Edna was hunched over one arm on her stomach and sucking her thumb. There was dried web of mucus on the rim of her nostril. As I came close she sniffed at the air and frowned.

Regina was turned away from the door. The covers were up to her ears and she was taking in the deep breaths of sleep.

I got into the bed softly, so lightly that hardly a spring creaked. The pain in my head throbbed with each heartbeat.

The green fluorescent arms of the clock next to my bed said three-thirty.

It was the first time I had been with another woman since we'd been married. And it was a prostitute. I didn't even like it. But I had gotten dark pleasure from that girl.

Whoever had killed Bonita Edwards had probably met her at Bethune Street. I imagined all the ways I could question Max. I imagined sapping him and waiting until he awoke, and then hitting him again. Maybe I wouldn't let him talk for hours. Maybe I never would.

At three-forty she said, "Did you get the money, Easy?"

"No, baby. I been askin' questions fo' Officer Naylor t'day. I ain't hadda chance t'look into it yet."

I thought that I'd make it look hard to get the money. I planned to tell Regina everything about my money after I was finished with the police.

I just needed time to get all the words straight.

I stayed very still in hopes that she'd lull back into sleep. I purged all thoughts of sex, violence, and death from my mind.

After a while I couldn't even remember what Marla looked like.

"You smell like you been in a whorehouse," she said at four-oh-five.

Neither one of us had moved.

"You know I love, you, Regina," I said.

"I know you think you do."

"You'n Edna mean more to me than anything."

"Uh-huh."

"Is that all you could say?"

I waited up until dawn but she never said another word.

TWELVE

MY TONGUE FELT like a cactus pad and the blood was pounding in my head. I got out of bed and walked along the walls into the living room.

They were all there.

Jesus was sitting in the light of the window reading a book and holding the fingers of his left hand against his head. I recognized his pose as the posture I took while reading.

Regina had on a turquoise housecoat. Edna, dressed only in diapers, sat in her lap. Mother and daughter sat staring at each other in awe. Just as I came into the room Edna reached for her mother's face and Regina leaned forward to be touched.

They were all so beautiful that I started to back away. But then somebody took the stairs in two steps and knocked at our door.

When Regina rose she saw me. A look of confusion crossed her face as if, maybe, I shouldn't have been there at all. Then she frowned and went to answer the door.

It was Gabby. She grinned at my daughter and wife, kissing them and making silly faces.

The smile died on her face when she saw me. I turned away and went back into the bedroom.

Regina came soon after saying, "You should be civil to Gabby Lee, Easy."

"Did she say somethin' to me?"

I noticed blood on the white pillowcase. The little Negro's memento from the night before. My right arm ached as I made to cover the pillow with the sheet.

"Gabby Lee had plenty of trouble with men, Easy. She might not know how to be civil to a man but that don't excuse you."

"Could I drive you today?"

Regina had taken off her robe and was about to step into her yellow dress.

"Why?"

"Like we used to do. Then I'll pick you up tonight."

"Why today?" She sounded suspicious.

"Listen, honey," I said. I put out my hand to zip her back. She hesitated a moment before allowing my touch. "I know I been wrong with you. I know that. But I wanna make it right."

"Yeah?"

"It's just that I gotta get through this thing with Quinten Naylor first."

She touched my ear where the blackjack had struck. "What happened to you?"

"I love you, Regina."

I sat down on the bed. My head hurt so much that it was past pain. It felt more like a kind of motion; like a razor-backed viper slithering through my brain. Regina saw the agony in my face and sat down next to me.

"What's wrong, baby?"

"I wanna drive you to work and I want you to do something for me too."

"What?"

"On October fourteenth you got a patient at the Temple emergency room. It was a boy named Gregory. I don't know his last name. I need to find out where he lives."

"What for?"

"He knew one'a them girls got killed."

"Why don't you just tell Quinten Naylor about it? He could find out himself."

"Maybe, but if I could come up with a name and an address then I would know for sure that Quinten could find him. You know the police make so much noise when they doin' anything and this Gregory might have a friend at Temple."

"But I need my car," Regina said.

"I'll pick you up at five, I swear I will."

"Well . . . I guess," she said finally. "But we gotta hurry if you wanna go. You know I got a timetable to keep."

Temple Hospital is a big gray building at the top of a hill on Temple Street. Edna was born there on a rainy January night. Regina was in a lot of pain during labor and the nurses were so nice that she decided to become a nurse's aide herself. She never worried about a profession before then. But you couldn't pry her away from that job with gold or honey.

I took a left turn before we came to the main entrance.

"What you doin'?" Regina asked.

"Parking. I thought we could get some coffee like we used to."

"I gotta get to work."

"It's only eight-thirty. You don't have to be on shift until nine-fifteen."

Regina shook her head. "I don't have the time this mornin'," she said.

I made a turn in the middle of the street and pulled into a loading zone in front of the main entrance.

Regina said, "You been off in yo' own thing all this time, baby. You know I got girlfriends in there who expect me to sit wit' them."

"But I'm your husband."

She patted my cheek, then kissed it. "I'll find out what I can about your emergency boy, honey. I'll call you 'round ten, okay?"

"I guess."

She kissed me on the lips and opened the door. I felt so bad to be alone that I almost called out to her. I watched her walk away. The moment she was out of the car her mind was fully on the job she had to do. She didn't look back. I waited until the large door she went through had closed.

By the time I was back home that razor-backed viper was boring at my skull. Gabby Lee and Edna were playing in the living room.

Jesus was packing his lunch in the kitchen.

"How you doin'?" I asked him.

Jesus looked up at me and smiled.

"Let me see your hands."

He flashed his palms at me quickly and then reached for his lunch bag. But I reached out to touch his shoulder.

"Let's have a good look now," I said.

He'd been eating something sticky in the last twenty-four hours. Mottled dirt ran down the seams between his fingers.

"You gotta wash your hands every night, Jesus Rawlins. If you go to bed like that you could attract ants, maybe even a rat."

Jesus glanced fearfully down at the floor.

"Go on now, wash up and get on down to school."

He ran to the bathroom.

I went back to bed counting heartbeats and breathing as slowly as I could.

When Gabby Lee started making loud cooing noises with Edna in the other room I shouted, "Cut out that noise! Cut it out!"

Edna began to cry. I wanted to go out there and hold my hand over her little mouth, but I knew it was the hangover. I knew it was all the guilt I felt over the whore and me. Me, the whore-man, the fool.

"Now you made that baby cry," Gabby Lee said from the bedroom door.

She had a hard stare for me but when I looked up into her eye she backed down. She backed all the way out of the room. I pulled myself from bed and cursed Quinten Naylor. I hated that man. If it wasn't for him I'd be fine. I actually believed that. Way past thirty and I was still a fool.

I went into Jesus' room with a denim bag and gathered up my clothes. Then I went to the bedroom to get the sheets.

Gabby Lee watched me silently as I went from room to room.

I made coffee and toast. I drank the brew but the toast went uneaten. I washed and shaved and then washed again. I said good morning to my baby girl when I was halfway human. She laughed and played with my fingers. It's a shame the way children will forgive parents their sins.

I didn't say another word to Gabby Lee. She went around the house sullenly hating me like she hated all men. But I couldn't blame her that morning. It seemed like I was on the warpath against women and that all the men I knew, and those I didn't know, were too. I treated Marla like a piece of meat. I wasn't honest with my wife and I yelled at my baby. Somebody was going around killing women and the police hardly cared until a white girl got it. I wasn't even sure that they cared about her.

The phone ringing nearly tore my head off. Gabby Lee didn't answer it. She wasn't going to be my secretary. The bell reminded me of machine-gun bursts. When I finally staggered up to it I had to restrain myself from throwing the goddam thing out of the window.

"Yeah," I whispered.

"Easy?" said Regina. "Is that you?"

"Uh-huh."

"His last name is Jewel and he lives at one sixty-eight Harpo. They said somebody really worked him over. All kinds of broken bones. Um. He got a young wife came and got him the next day."

"Thanks, babe," I said. I'd written down the address and name on the tabletop in the dining room. Gabby Lee stared daggers at me but she didn't say a word.

"Easy?" Regina asked.

"Yeah?"

"Do you like doin' this?"

"Doin' what?"

"This. This workin' with the cops an' lookin' for people like this boy."

"Uh-uh, no, baby. I just wanna be home with you. That's what I like."

There was a neighborhood tomcat stalking across the front lawn. I was watching him through the front window when all of a sudden he froze and stared at me from a half-crouch. His eyes were Regina's, staring through my lies.

"But you do it 'cause you have to?"

"What?"

"I had to have me a baby. I had to. I like this job and I like a lotta things but I had to have Edna. I'd die without her."

"I'd die without you, honey," I said.

"I gotta go now, Easy. You be here at five?"

"Yeah. I'll be there."

When I went out the front door L.A. was waiting for me. You could see as far as the mountains would let you. I didn't deserve it, but it was mine just the same.

THIRTEEN

GREGORY JEWEL LIVED in a California-style tenement. The project was a deep lot with a row of white-and-green bungalows facing each other. At the end of the aisle of sixteen dwellings was a solitary bungalow. That was Gregory Jewel's house. A little bronze tab over the door buzzer said "assistant manager."

A young woman opened the door. She had light brown skin with dark brown freckles around her broad nose. She had spaces between her teeth which enhanced her smile and you could see that she always smiled. Even when she was sad she smiled. Her eyes were wet and there were creases in her young face, the creases of days of crying. Her solemn, creased face told of how she'd look when she became an older woman—Gregory would be a lucky man if he held on to her that long.

"Yes?" she said.

"Gregory Jewel," I said in a gruff tone. The hangover was talking for me.

"No, sir. No Gregory Jewel here."

"Com'on, honey. I know this is his house. An' I know Greg ain't goin' nowhere 'cause he's all beat up. So tell'im that Easy Rawlins is here an' unless he wants the police on'im he better talk wit' me now."

She listened to my speech patiently and when I finished she said, "Sorry, mistah, but they ain't no Gregory Jewel in this house."

"Ella!" came a shout from the house.

"What?"

"Who is that?"

"Just some man lookin' fo'a Gregory Jewel. I told'im that they wasn't any here."

"Come on back here," the voice shouted.

Ella closed the door in my face. I took it. I felt like pushing past her and dragging Gregory from wherever he was hiding but I kept the anger caged. I was saving it for a stronger foe.

When the door opened again Ella's smile was gone.

"Com'on," she said.

The rooms in the bungalow were like a ship's cabin. There was hardly enough space to turn around. The furniture was mismatched and the linoleum on the floor was rotted around the corners. There was a professional photograph of Ella in the arms of a skinny, buck-toothed man tacked to the wall. There was a hot plate and a stack of dishes next to the front door.

Through that room was an even tinier bedroom. There was probably a toilet in a closet off from there. I never found out though, because the buck-toothed man was laid up in the small bed.

Gregory's left arm went straight out to the side and was wrapped, up past the shoulder, in a thick white cast. His right hand was bandaged and both of his feet were in casts. The casts were all scuffed and frayed. There was a bandage around Gregory's head and there was blood in both of his eyes.

"What you want?" he asked.

There was only enough room for a squat upholstered chair with their bed. I sat in it and Ella slumped against the door.

"You Gregory Jewel?"

My official tone made him nervous.

"How come?" he asked.

I looked at him for a few seconds. I didn't feel sorry for the man, because he called this misery on himself. But I felt kindred to his misery. It seemed to me that my whole life had been spent walking into shabby little houses with poor people bleeding or hacking or just dying quietly under the weight of our "liberation." I was born in a house no larger than that one. I lived there with two half sisters and one stepbrother. I watched my mother die of pneumonia on a bed like Gregory's.

All of a sudden my hangover was gone. I took a deep breath of sour air and said, "I gotta know 'bout how you was beaten, man."

"How come? You a cop?"

"The cops will be here 'less you tell me sumpin'."

"How I know that?"

"Listen, I ain't gonna mess around wit'you. If you want the cops here I'll send'em. I need t'know 'bout how you got messed up. They do too."

The young couple looked at each other, then Gregory asked, "What's up?"

"This is deep, Greg. Real deep. You don't want yo' name

nowhere around it. You could take that from me. I ain't gonna tell ya nuthin', but it's better fo'you that way. Now this is the last time I'm gonna ask it. After this I'm gone an' ev'rybody gonna know yo' name."

Gregory tried to laugh. "Wasn't nuthin'. Ain't nuthin' t'tell. I run inta him at a bar an' he said sumpin' I didn't like."

"What about Juliette LeRoi? I heard that the fight was over her."

Ella opened the door and went out.

"What you wanna go an' do that fo', man?" Gregory squealed. "That ain't right."

"What about Juliette LeRoi?" I asked again. I took a twenty-dollar bill from my pocket and put it on the cast.

Only great concentration kept Gregory from snatching that bill with the two available fingers of his bandaged hand. "What you wanna know?"

"What happened with you that night you got beat up?"

Gregory looked away from me at the small window near the top of the low ceiling. He brought to mind a chick that had fallen from the nest.

"I know'er. That's all. I went with'er down to Aretha's t'get some drinks. We did that sometimes and then maybe I'd get some, you know what I mean?

"So there was this dude with a beard there an' he said that he wanted her t'come wit' him. I stood up an' he pushed me across the room. Then he goes out the door pullin' on Julie. I got a bad temper so I runs on out an' goes after'em. But he grabs me an' th'ows me in the alley." Tears came to Gregory's face. "First he broke my arm, man. Then he stomped my feet. Doctor said I might not even be able to walk right, an' you know we get our rent free if I look after things here an' they gonna throw us out if I don't get back to it soon."

"What about the man an' Juliette?" I didn't want to hear about his problems. There was nothing I could do.

"She saved me, man. She yelled at'im an' pulled him back. I mean, he let her pull him. He was big an' real strong. He hit me in the head a couple of times with a trash can. The last I seen they was goin' off together."

"She call'im anything?"

"She did but I don't remember." Gregory shook his head but that hurt him so he winced.

"Did he pull her away?"

"Uh-uh. She said she'd go with'im if he let up."

"That's all?"

"He sounded funny."

"Like what?"

"He'd say 'mon' instead'a 'man.' He almost sounded like he was a English nigger."

That was enough for me. I stood up to go and Gregory said, "What's this all about?"

"You don't know?"

"Know what? What should I know?"

"Juliette is dead. She got killed sometime after she went off with this dude who busted you up."

"Naw, uh-uh, Julie ain't dead." Gregory gave a little laugh to prove it.

"Don't you talk to nobody, man?" I asked.

"Ella's all since this." He raised his broken arm about three inches.

I left him there to lie in his coffin-sized bedroom and consider how close he had come to death.

Ella was on the matchbook sofa crying when I left. I didn't say anything to her. There's no cure for living a life of poverty. There's nothing to say either.

Willa Scott had lived with her parents on Eighty-third Street. They were two small people who owned a modest house. They'd had Willa late in life and were now of retirement age. All they could do was ask me why. "Why would somebody do that to our girl?"

"Did she ever have friends come to the house?" I asked. "Men friends."

Her mother, a hen-shaped woman, shook her head. The father, who never got out of his chair as long as I was there, said, "She was kinda private. She told us that most a these men she meets out there wasn't good enough t'bring on home. But you know she was gonna get a job for the schools. She said she was."

"Did she know a man, a Negro man with a beard?"

"No sir," Mrs. Scott answered. "Did you want to see the pictures of her?"

Mrs. Scott brought out a handmade photograph album. She and her husband beamed at the photos while I stood behind them. She kneeled at his side and they both cooed and clucked.

I thanked them about halfway through.

When I went through the front door they were still admiring Willa's memory.

FOURTEEN

BETWEEN EIGHTY-SIXTH STREET and Eighty-seventh Place on Central Avenue, not far from the Scotts' house, was a long stucco building that we called Hollywood Row. It was nowhere near Hollywood but we called it that because of its showy residents. It was only two stories high but it took up the whole length of the block. The bottom floor was made up of a mom-and-pop store called Market, two liquor stores, three bars, and a Chinese laundry called Lin Chow. The upper floor was a long hall of studio apartments populated by transient gangsters, whores, and musicians who'd seen their day come and go. The musicians were the only long-term residents. Lips McGee, a man I'd known since I was a youngster in Houston, had lived there for thirteen years.

First I went to Lin Chow, where a small woman wearing a

blue quilted jacket and red cotton pants was ironing. She looked at me and gave me a toothless grin. I handed her the denim bag and she emptied it on the counter. She jotted something down on a white pad and tore the slip off for me.

I couldn't read it.

"How long?" I shouted.

She held up two fingers and shouted back, "Two day."

"Today?" I pointed at the floor indicating now.

She shook her head and held up two fingers again.

I used her sign language as a kind of omen and went to one of the liquor stores, where I purchased two pints of Johnnie Walker Red Label scotch.

The only entrance to the dwellings of Hollywood Row was a rickety door that opened into an alley behind the building. To the left of the door there was a corral of trash cans breeding ants, roaches, and flies. The cans were all overflowing with aluminum TV dinner plates and liquor bottles. The wooden stairs were spongy. The long hall was covered with a carpet that once was green. Now it was simply edged with color like a dry brown riverbed with dying grasses along its banks.

Hollywood Row wasn't a private place. People treated it like one big house. Most of the studio apartment doors were open. One door I passed revealed a man fully dressed in an antique zoot suit and a white ten-gallon hat. As I passed by we regarded each other as two wary lizards might stare as they slithered across some barren stone.

There were smells of cooking and incense and various human odors. And then there was a long and clear note made by a silver trumpet. The note broke into a ripple of sounds that somehow ended up at the same clear cry. And then came an earthy "wah-wah" that drowned out all the mortality in that hall.

I followed the sound to a door toward the end of the hall. On my way I passed shabby scenes of men and women in various states of undress. Some were lovers oblivious of my passage. Others were looking for someone to come down that hall and deliver them from their lives.

Lips McGee's door was ajar. I knocked gently and his trumpet answered, "Wah?"

"It's me, Lips, Easy Rawlins," I said.

"Com'on in, Easy."

The room wasn't big but it was larger than Gregory Jewel's whole house. There was a couch, a maple table with two oak chairs, and a sink over which a window peeked out onto Central Avenue. The walls were all covered with photographs of Lips' life. The larger ones were of him and the jazz greats. But there were older, brownish pictures of him playing in the one-room clubs and jazz parades down in Houston. He was old by then but in his heyday Lips was what every black man wanted to be. He was dapper and self-assured, articulate, and had money in his pocket. He was always surrounded by beautiful women, but what really made me jealous was the way he looked when he played his horn.

He'd stand straight and tall and play that horn as if every bit of his soul could be concentrated through a silver pipe. Sweat shone across his wide forehead and his eyes became shiny slits. When Lips hit the high notes he made that horn sound like a woman who was where she wanted to be when she was in love with you.

The smell of marijuana permeated the room. Lips was standing next to the sink; he'd probably been serenading the street. He wore blue jeans and a yellow T-shirt that hung loose on his bony frame. His hair was longish and combed backwards. His orangy-brown chin was whiskered with black and white stubs.

"Wah-wah," he blew. And then, "What you doin' here, Easy Rawlins?"

I sat down in one of the chairs.

"Makin' a social call," I said.

Lips laughed. He took a plate of something that looked like chili-out-of-a-can from the stove and placed it across from me on the table. Far away I heard sirens, lots of sirens. They were police sirens, not fire trucks.

"That's what the snake say t'the hare when he comin' down his hole," Lips said.

"What's that?"

" 'Makin' a social call." Lips chuckled. "An' the first thing he do is eat his host."

"That might be," I said. "But I ain't hungry t'night." I took a pint bottle from my jacket pocket. Lips grinned a little wider.

"I see," the old man said.

He brought out two jelly jars and filled them with my scotch. He blew a kiss to his glass before sipping. Then he smiled up at the ceiling.

Lips told me stories that I'd heard a hundred times before but I still laughed heartily. When we got quiet Lips would take a sip of whiskey, then a bite of chili. Then he'd blow a few notes, maybe even the beginning of a song—a nursery rhyme or jazz hit. He asked me about Mouse and Dupree Bouchard and Jackson Blue.

After we cracked the seal on the second bottle, Lips asked, "What you want here wit' me, man?"

"You hear 'bout these women gettin' killed?"

"Yeah?"

"I'm lookin' around with Quinten Naylor to find out who did it."

"Uh-huh?"

"One'a them girls, the last one, was called Robin Garnett in the newspaper, but the name she used down here was Cyndi Starr."

For a moment the old man looked even older. Then he licked his lips.

"Yeah," he said. "That white girl lived down here sometimes. I wondered where she went. Cyndi Starr, I wonder where you are, baby. I wonder wonder where." He smiled a different, softer smile for her memory.

"You knew her?" I asked.

When Lips looked me in the eye I knew he was going to go off on what we used to call his "wild talk." But that was the only way he knew how to say what he meant, so I took another drink and wished that I had been seated on the more comfortable couch.

"I been here thirteen years and there ain't never been no change. I mean, somebody moves out but then someone just like him, or her or what-have-you, moves in and it's the same. It's like you get so high like in a dream where you flyin', an' sometimes you think, 'What am I doin' up here?' And you go crashin' down on the ground, an' sometimes you don't even care. 'Cause nuthin' matters when a wave pulls out. The sand smooths over any footprint that was there.

"You ast me if I know Cyndi Starr but you ain't askin' 'bout Hilda Wildheart. You ain't askin' 'bout Curtis Mayhew. You know what happened t'them?"

I shook my head.

"Same fuckin' thing. Same fuckin' thing. They gone. Gone. That's all she wrote fo'them. Beautiful girl all sad inside want some man t'make her feel good. Put on some silky clothes an' some makeup. All the wolves up an' down the street make some noise an' she fo'get how bad she feel. Whas wrong with that? Huh? Whas wrong?"

There wasn't an answer.

"Hilda Wildheart, Sonia Juarez, Yakeesha Lewis . . ." He counted them off on his fingers as he went. "Tiffany Marlowe, even yo' Lois Chan been up here. Broken hearts, broken jaws, broken necks. All the pussy you could ever wanna be 'round. You know, mo' than one'a them girls kept me company when I was so low I couldn't even go outside. They brew some tea an' love me. Yeah," he shrugged, "they mighta lifted five bucks after I was asleep but they didn't take it all. Uh-uh. Them girls was all beautiful, an' here you go askin' 'bout Cyndi Starr like this is the first thing you know 'about them po' girls. Young boys like you come up here t'get some pussy an' that's it. You gone."

Lips shrugged again. I poured him another glass of whiskey.

"She come up here laughin' an' singin' with her girlfriends an' her boyfriends," Lips said. I knew that he was talking about Cyndi because now he seemed to be talking to me rather than at me. "She used to come in here an' tell me things till even my old dick would get hard. She liked to say how she could handle two men till they was like jelly. She had a foul mouth but she was so sweet sometimes."

"When was the last time she was here?"

"Maybe I seen'er about three weeks ago. She was gone for a while before that."

"Gone where?"

"She was just gone there fo'while. She had this other white girl stayin' there. Sylvia."

"How long was she gone?"

"I dunno. Three, four months. 'Bout that. Maybe more."

"What was this Sylvia girl like?"

"Raven. Long raven hair and black eyes and white skin so pale that it was always a shock t'look at her."

"Where's she now?"

Lips shook his head. "Don't know that either. She stayed a couple'a days when Cyndi got back but then she went. That was 'bout two months ago. Yeah, them girls was thick."

"Cyndi have a job?"

"She'd take off her clothes down at Melodyland."

"What room was hers?"

"The purple. Three doors down on the other side."

I thanked him for his help and toasted his virility.

Before I left he said, "You drinkin' pretty heavy there, boy. Better slow it down some."

"I got a lot on my mind, old man. Too much."

"You ain't gonna have much of a mind left if you keep on like that."

I laughed. "I'm still young, Lips. I can take it."

"I seen men turn old in six months under that bottle, man. I seen 'em die in a year."

I used my pocketknife, pried open the lock with no trouble.

Cyndi Starr's room had no history. Everything was right then. The single mattress on the floor in the corner. The signed photographs of Little Richard and Elvis Presley tacked to the wall. There were three partially eaten cans of pork and beans in the sink, each one with a spoon handle sticking out. A cardboard box made her night table. The Formica-top dining table was covered with movie magazines and one hard-cover book. That was a thick brown tome entitled *Industrial Psychology*.

"Can I help you?" The voice behind me was musical and delicate.

When I turned I was met by a small, fair man. His skin was almost white. He had a sparse goatee, long eyelashes, and brown suede pants and shirt. His shoes were made from blue fake alligator skin.

"No," I told him.

He cocked his head to the side and looked me up and down with a hint of a smile on his lips. He met my eye and blinked slowly. "Then what you doin' in here?"

"Lookin' fo' Cyndi."

He looked around the room. "She ain't here. An' even if she was, why you be openin' her do' if she don't answer?"

I was nervous in front of this brazen little man. His frank stares and insinuating smiles, coupled with the alcohol, made me uncomfortable.

"Ain't you heard, man?" I asked.

"Heard what?" His eyes hardened into the question.

"She's dead. Murdered by the man been killin' them girls."

"No." His lower lip trembled. He clasped his hands and took a step toward me.

"Raped her and brutalized her and then mutilated her body." I nodded. I felt better now that my inquisitor was disturbed.

He took another step and grabbed my sleeve.

"No," he said again. His eyes were begging me.

"An' I'm here fo' the police . . ."

He didn't give me enough time to finish. The little man stepped away from me, putting his hands on his thighs. His face was hard and unyielding. He backed straight to the door and then turned. He was gone in less than three heartbeats.

I looked around a little bit more. I found a yearbook from Los Angeles High School, the class of '55, and a folder full of *professional* photos of Cyndi. In one shot she posed naked, except for a G-string and her fingertips, feigning surprise on an empty stage. The spot light on her was in the shape of a butterfly against the black back drop. The White Butterfly. In a corner there was a box of clothes. She had everything in there, from a UCLA letter sweater to a pair of glitter-encrusted high heels.

I studied another of the photos for a while. It was her looking over her bare shoulder at the camera. The face was hard and beautiful. She wasn't healthy in that photograph. None of the force or sensuality in that snarl appeared in her college photo. I understood why no one but John had recognized her. Cyndi Starr was a different woman on Hollywood Row.

I felt like a child's pallbearer going down the stairs with her box of memories.

FIFTEEN

CALLED THE POLICE station from a phone booth in the street. Quinten agreed to wait for me at his office. He was all starch and good manners.

When I was going up the stairs to the station door I saw five men coming down. Four of them were policemen surrounding Roger Vaughn. He was manacled, hand and foot. He looked up at me and I remembered all the sirens I'd heard at Hollywood Row.

When Roger saw me he put both hands out to me. Instinctively I reached out too. But two of the cops clubbed him. He slumped down and they dragged him off to a van in the street.

The desk sergeant knew who I was and waved me by as I went up to him. But I stopped to ask, "What they got that man out there for?"

"Double killing. He found some guy on top of his wife."

By that time Quinten had his own office with a clouded glass door that had his name and rank stenciled on it in green paint. I lifted my hand but he must have recognized the shadow against the pane.

"Come on in, Ezekiel," he said.

It had been two days and he was five years older. His cannon-ball shoulders sagged down a little further and his head tilted to the side as if he found it too heavy to keep erect. When I came into the room he sighed like a dogface at the end of a thirty-mile forced march.

"You look half dead, Q-man," I said, coining the nickname that was to follow him the rest of his life.

"And you're drunk," was his reply.

"It's a hard world out there, brother. A little booze keeps ya from sinkin' to the bottom of the barrel."

"What do you want?"

"I'm feeling generous, officer. I've come to share what I know with you-all." I took a seat in a chair set by the door.

"What's that?"

"Them first three women was killed just about two weeks apart, right?"

Quinten nodded and his eyes drooped as if he might nod off on me.

"But then this Robin Garnett is dead just a couple days after you find Bonita Edwards."

"Yes, you're right about that," Naylor said in his prim Philadelphia accent. "Not only that. She was white, she was a college student, and she didn't live anywhere near this neighborhood; no one seems to know what she was doing down here. That's one of the reasons the brass is so upset. They think some crazy Negro is going to go on a rampage killing white women."

"Yeah." I smiled. "But I don't think you got it all. You see, this li'l darlin' got kilt wasn't all so pure as some might wanna think."

"What's that mean?"

I threw down one of Cyndi's stripper photographs.

Naylor studied it for a minute.

"Why didn't anybody show me this?"

"Nobody knew, man. That picture in the *Times* an' *Examiner* didn't look nuthin' like this stripper. An' mosta the people knew her prob'ly don't buy the mo'nin' news no way. An' even if they did, why they wanna come down here when you prob'ly th'ow them in jail fo'bad thoughts?"

"Where'd you get this?" Maybe he was going to throw *"me"* in the slam.

"At her pad, man. You know the Hollywood Row, right?"

"How'd you know where to go, Easy?"

"Listen." I held up my palm for him to admire. "I got my secrets. That's why you need me."

Quinten looked at me hard for a minute.

Finally he said, "All right. I'll go look into it. Makes it a little neater for us. I don't know what the man's going to think, though. You know they get real upset when these white women cross the line."

"Why don't we drive on down to where that girl's parents are at? You know, just for some questions. We could bring that picture down there an' see what they got say." I didn't mention the box of belongings I had out in the car.

"Why?"

"It just don't smell right, Quinten. Why she get killed two days after the other one when they gettin' murdered ev'ry two weeks or more 'fore that? How come this is a white one an' all the rest'a them is black? An' how come they kill this coed an' they killin' B-girls all before this?"

"You got the proof here that she was one of those kind of women."

He held up the photograph to prove his point.

"Yeah," I said. "But maybe that's not the girl he killed."

"What?" Quinten slammed the picture down on his desk.

"I mean, it's the same body, the same life, but it was Robin Garnett got killed, not Cyndi Starr. I mean, they found her all dressed up like a coed, right? If it was the coed who was killed and not the stripper, then maybe there was some other reason fo'the murder, right?"

"Maybe the killer knew her. Maybe he knew about her double life." Quinten didn't want any complications.

"Yeah, I guess. He knew Juliette LeRoi, all right."

"What's that?"

I told him about the fight at Aretha's and Gregory Jewel. Also about how Bonita Edwards didn't know the other girls.

"You got all this and you're just coming in here now?"

"Hey, man, calm down. I'm here. Pass what I told you to your partner an' then let's you an' me go over to see the Garnetts."

"I don't think so. I appreciate you wanting to help, but police work should be kept in the house. They have enough trouble with a Negro cop. What are they going to think about you?"

I didn't like the way he said that. "What do you think about me, Quinten?"

A sneer flashed across Quinten's face. He sat forward placing his big fists on the desk. "I think you're rotten, Mr. Rawlins. You and your friend Raymond Alexander. Both of you belong in the penitentiary. But nobody wants to make that a priority. Everybody's always got something better. Maybe you'll help us catch this guy, probably you will. But whoever he is, he's just crazy. He can't help it. But you could. You're a criminal, Ezekiel Rawlins.

I might have to work with you, I do have to. But just because you have to wipe your ass doesn't mean that you have to love shit."

Maybe if I hadn't been drinking it wouldn't have hurt. I don't know. But everybody was on me. Regina and Gabby Lee and Quinten Naylor. I felt like I needed a drink. I did need a drink.

The Los Angeles phone book was my best friend in those days. I went north to Pico Boulevard and then west until I hit Hauser. The Garnetts were five blocks further north from there.

They lived in a two-story Spanish-style house that shared a large lawn with a weeping willow and sloppy-looking St. Bernard on a long chain. The whole yard was surrounded by a low cement fence that had been treated to look like adobe. The roof was made from curved red tiles. Terra-cotta. Probably imported from Mexico or maybe even Italy. Two sharkish-looking Caddies were parked in the driveway. Five boy's bicycles were parked on the lawn.

I took the sweater, the yearbook, and the envelope of her working photos and put them in a large brown paper bag. Then I went up to the door and pressed the button. A buzzer went off in the house. That surprised me. I expected bells, Spanish bells to toll or chime, at least to ring. A buzzer was what you heard in a hardware store.

A boy in his early teens swung the door open wide. He was still young enough to have feminine features and so greatly resembled his dead sister's photographs. His face darkened for a moment when he saw me. Maybe he was expecting one of his little boyfriends rambling up on a J. C. Higgins.

"Hi." He had a beautiful all-American-boy grin.

"I'm lookin' fo' your mother or father." I smiled too.

"Dad's out but Mom's here. I'll get her."

"Mom!" he shouted as soon as he was out of sight.

He left the door open, either out of trust or ignorance, and I could see clear through the house. The living room was sunken and plush with white furry furniture. The back wall was mostly glass and looked out into the patio, backyard, and swimming pool.

The white woman, who was scolding the boy as she made her way from the patio, wasn't much older than I. But she seemed to have weathered many years. Mothers age more quickly than fathers do.

She was tall for a woman and erect. She wore a midcalf one-piece dress that was green with little horses printed in a spiral line from her neck to the hem. I could tell that the dress was expensive because the pattern wasn't askew. Somebody paid attention when they sewed it.

"Yes?" she asked. Her smile was tentative.

"Mrs. Garnett?"

"Yes?" Her hand moved toward the doorknob.

"My name is Easy, Easy Rawlins," I said.

"If you're from one of the papers, I'm sorry but we're not giving interviews. We . . ." She pulled the door close to her side and moved forward.

"No ma'am, I found some things that belong to you."

"I'm sorry, Mr. Rawlins, but I haven't lost anything."

As she made ready to shut the door I said, "Your daughter's things, ma'am."

"What are you talking about?" Her face and voice would have made a good final Friday scene on *As the World Turns*.

"She lived down in my neighborhood. Down on Central Avenue, and she left some clothes an' pictures down there."

"You're mistaken, sir. My daughter lived right here."

"No, ma'am. I mean, maybe she did, but she lived down on Central too. I got her things right here in this bag."

When I pulled the blue sweater out of the bag she cried, "Oh my God!" and ran back into the house.

She yelled, "Milo! Milo!" and then she ran back to the door.

"Who are you?"

It hurt to look in her eyes, so I stared at the mint weed that had pressed its way through the cracks at the base of the wall. I didn't want to be there but I'd be damned if I could question black people and not white ones.

The boy and a few of his friends ran to her side. Actually they came up behind her.

"Mom," Milo said.

"Go on back to your room, honey." She was in control again. She turned and led them away from the door and came back.

"Who are you?"

"I'm Easy Rawlins, ma'am, and I've been helping the police since your daughter's death."

"You're a policeman?" She didn't sound relieved.

"No exactly, ma'am. But I've been working with them. Some Negro women have also been killed and I know the neighborhood. I just wanted to ask you a couple of questions about these things I found."

"Excuse me, Mr. Rawlins," she said with a perfect facsimile of a smile. "I've been upset, you can imagine. Come in and show me what you have."

I let her lead me into the sunken living room and took a seat on the furry couch.

"Can I get you something?" she asked.

"No. Just lemme show what I got here." I was less sure of my convictions now that I was in the house with her. She was no longer some white person put out of bounds by a racist world. She'd become a mother who had lost a child and I was on the verge of making that injury worse.

"We have pop and milk and beer," she recited. It was her regular list for a guest.

"I'd take a beer."

She squared her shoulders and turned for a door near the glass wall.

"All right," she said. "I'll just be a minute."

She went quickly through the door.

I looked at my watch. She was gone for six minutes.

She came back with a platter on which sat a soda-fountain glass full of amber brew. She smiled and put the platter in front of me.

"Did you know my daughter?" she asked. She probably wanted to wail.

"No, ma'am."

I empited the bag on the table before us. She had taken a seat on the couch at an angle so that she faced me. She was a brave woman, I'll hand her that.

She picked up the high school yearbook and pressed it between her two hands. She looked for a moment at the letters. I was getting nervous. She got to the envelope of photographs. At first she looked quizzical. Like, "What could Robin have wanted with these?" But then the avalanche fell. She threw the photographs on the floor.

Her breaths started to come in sharp little gasps. I could almost hear her bird's heart.

She swallowed and brought both hands to the back of her neck. Before her lay a patchwork, in photographs, of her daughter's life. A come-on smile, a bare breast. A sinuous pose that made her mother sit even straighter. The White Butterfly.

"Why?" Her voice was so full of feeling that it took me a moment to decipher the word.

"Ma'am?" I said after a while.

And, after another wait, "Ma'am?"

"Yes?"

"Is that Robin?"

She didn't deny it.

"Didn't the police ask you what she did on the weekends, ma'am? Did you know?"

"Would you like something to drink, Mr., Mr. . . ." She turned her body fully toward me. I was sure that if she'd turned her neck her head would have twisted off and shattered on the floor.

"Sure," I said.

She got up slowly and went back into the kitchen. My beer still sat on the table—untouched.

After about fifteen minutes I looked in on her. The kitchen was white linoleum and waxed maple. She was sitting at the table with her head cradled in her arms.

SIXTEEN

I HAD TO ask about Cyndi. Maybe it made sense that she was killed by this man. Maybe it did.

But when I left that house I was finished with the case. Quinten and the police had my best shot. The bearded man was a good candidate for the killings. And I had a life to get back to.

I could hear Mofass hacking before I was halfway up the stairs. When I came into the room I found him holding his chest and breathing hard.

He looked up at me with hangdog, yellowy eyes. His lips formed a crooked grimace. There was a cigar between the fingers of his left hand.

"Sick," he whispered.

Mofass lolled back like wounded sea lion. The skin around his lips was ashen. He wheezed instead of breathed. His eyes were focused somewhere outside the room.

I'd seen dead men that looked healthier.

"We better get you a doctor, man," I said. I even reached for the phone.

"What for?"

He took a shallow breath and opened his eyes wide as saucers. Then he stifled a cough. He revved his lungs for a few moments, then said, "Just gimme a minute. I be okay."

"You need a doctor."

"I need to pay the rent. That's what I need."

He got up by leaning against the desk and pushing himself up. He stood by holding the chair and then the wall. When he went through the small door that led to his toilet I wondered if he would die in there.

A tiny black ant was foraging among the crumbs and ashes of Mofass' desk. I put my finger next to him. He crawled all along the crevices between my fingers. I watched him and marveled that some god watched me like that. I got the urge to crush the insect but just then the toilet flushed and Mofass came banging into the room.

His face was cleaned up and his eyes were alive again. There was a waver in his walk but he didn't hold on to anything.

"We gonna go?" he asked me.

The building we went to was called the Dorado, deep in Culver City. The walls were yellow plaster edged by weathered timbers. Terra-cotta pots lined the walkway to the front door. Each one overflowed with serpentine vines. The door said "DeCampo Associates."

A round-faced Japanese woman sat at a round desk in the middle of a large entrance. She was placid and fat and golden. Her eyes went from Mofass to me.

"Afternoon, Mrs. Narataki," Mofass said.

She smiled wider and looked him in the eye.

"Are they here?" Mofass nodded at the large oak door behind her.

Mrs. Narotaki said, "Have a seat. I'll tell them."

There were large red velvet chairs near the front door. Mofass and I went to them and sat side by side.

The small table next to me held a crystal vase that held seven white tulips. The ceiling was high and painted with a counterfeit Renaissance scene. There was a light blue sky complete with cotton-candy clouds and fat-boy angels with fig leaves to keep them modest.

"I want you to follow the program here, Mo," I whispered.

"Don't worry, Mr. Rawlins, I know what to do. But you got to remember that these here people in business t'make money. They ain't got no time t'be worried 'bout any li'l ole thang."

"Like what?"

"The Bontemps family."

The Bontempses were an elderly couple who lived in one of my apartment buildings. The Magnolia Street Apartments. They were in their eighties and their only son was dead. I let them pay me what they could for the rent and accepted the rest in labor. Of course, there was only so much that they could do in advanced age. Henry watered the lawn and swept the front porch every day. Crystal kept tabs on neighbors who might have wanted to skip the rent by moving out in the middle of the night. She was insomniac, so every night noise drove her from her bed.

"I can't help what I do, Mofass. If I gots to give a man a break, that's what I do. I done it for you."

He swallowed deeply.

"Anyway, I just want you to tell'em what we agreed on. Okay?"

"Yes sir."

Mofass lost all sense when it came to money. Money was his god and it wasn't a kindly deity.

Mrs. Narotaki looked up from her desk and smiled. "You can go in now."

The first thing you saw when going through the door was the garden. The ceiling-to-floor windows of the opposite wall looked out on a large garden with an Olympic-sized marble pond at its center. Two snowy swans preened at the center of the pond. The glass was tinted, which made the sky seem a deeper shade of blue. Mature willows trailed their sad leaves across the grounds, and a large white rabbit held one ear aloft as he nibbled in the grass and stared into the window.

The room was large and sunny. The walls were covered with paintings. The kind of paintings old European lords had made to glorify their possessions. There was a small scene of dead game hung upside down from a peg on a wall. Below the fowl and hares an attentive hunting dog sat. Behind him a rifle leaned against the wall.

A voluptuous maid carried a jug of milk and smiled from one frame. A white servant stood in a fancy den in another.

There were stuffed chairs against the wall like the chairs we had outside. But the room was dominated by a long ash table that was surrounded by six wooden chairs. Four of the chairs were already occupied.

"Mr. Wharton," one of the men said. He sat nearest the door

and rose to shake Mofass' hand. He was short, simply dressed in a yellow cardigan sweater and dark brown slacks. His shirt was a cotton pullover with three buttons at the throat.

Mofass grinned and nodded. "Mr. Vie," he said. "I'd like you to meet Mr. Ezekiel Rawlins. Mr. Rawlins is one of the men who works for me. He also has a small share in that property you're interested in."

Mofass took my elbow and guided it until the little white man and I were shaking hands.

His eyes were a grayish blue. They told me that he was very happy to meet me and that we should be friends.

"Very happy to meet you, Mr. Rawlins," he said.

I was ushered into a seat between Mr. Vie and Mofass. Over the table Mofass and I were introduced to the other men, who all leaned over to shake our hands.

There was Fargo Baer, a big man in a proper brown suit. He had red hair everywhere. It was manageable and short on his head but it sprouted like weeds from his ears and throat and even from the backs of his hands.

Next to Fargo sat Bernard Seavers. Bernard was skinny, shifty-eyed, and bone-colored. His thick black hair made him look as if he were wearing a hat.

Finally, at the head of the table sat Jack DeCampo. Jack was the leader. His skin was olive-colored and smooth. His eyes were any light color you wanted them to be.

He formed his long fingers into a tent that met at its apex between his eyes and looked at Mofass for a long time.

Then he looked at me. "It's a pleasure to meet you, sir."

I nodded shyly and ducked my head in reverence. It was the way I used to grease white men in the south.

"We represent an investment syndicate interested in real estate."

The rest of the men, including Mofass, were like hungry jays eyeing a newly seeded lawn.

"Mr. Rawlins owns less than five percent of the property you're interested in, gentlemen. But since he and I work together I figured that he'd do well to hear what we had to say here." Mofass could talk like a white man when he had to.

DeCampo smiled at me.

"We're glad to have you here."

I grinned as foolishly as I could.

"We think we can help you, Mr. Wharton," Bernard Seavers said. The focus left me as soon as they knew how worthless I was. Five percent wouldn't stand in their way. If Mofass wanted to impress his hired hand they didn't mind.

"We want to make you money," Mr. Vie chirped.

"You'll have to pardon me if I don't believe you," Mofass said. He knew what I wanted. He knew how to squeeze.

"I know it sounds strange, Mr. Wharton," DeCampo said. "But our interests have crossed here."

"You mean about that property I got over on Willoughby?"

"You have the land. We have the capital." He put his hands together and pressed.

"What do you get out of this? Interest on a loan?"

His laugh was the sizzle of acid on skin. "Well, maybe a little more than that."

"How much more?"

"We get seventy-five percent of the corporation we make here. You sit back and let the money roll in."

"Seventy-five percent?"

"Yes, Mr. Wharton," Mr. Vie put in. "We're bringing in the capital and also the information that will make that investment most lucrative."

I could see the swans flirting. They stirred up the water so that it threw off powerful flashes of the afternoon sun.

"What is this information?"

Mr. DeCampo smiled. "The county is going to make Willoughby into a main street. Five lanes wide. And almost all of your nine acres will still be intact after the construction."

"So the value of the property will go up then?" Mofass asked. I could tell by the way he asked that he understood why I didn't want to sell before.

"In ten years it will be worth more than all of us here in this room could raise. We're talking supermarkets and department stores, Mr. Wharton. Maybe an office building in the future. Who knows?"

"But if we just wait, wouldn't the property be its own collateral?" Mofass asked innocently.

The jays started fidgeting. There was suddenly danger in the room.

"I mean," Mofass continued, "why should we take this kind of deal when we could own everything ourselves?"

"The truth is," Fargo Baer said, "we're letting you in on the ground floor with this information. The land is unzoned now. As soon as the county planner lays out the new construction, the council is going to limit what you can do. I mean, you could push something through if you wanted, but it will cost you a prime penny then."

"And," Bernard Seavers put in. "Letting the banks know about the plans would cause other development projects. Right now we have the jump on everybody. Whatever we build will make us the business center of the neighborhood."

"So you wouldn't want us to tell anybody about this here meeting?" Mofass asked.

"Our partners wouldn't like that," DeCampo said as pleasantly as he could.

"And just who is that?"

The acid hiss issued from his mouth again. Then, "Men who know about land sales and new roads. Men who don't like to be cheated."

"But it's cheating to use this information to make a profit, ain't it? It's my taxes building that road?"

"In five years your twenty-five percent will be worth a million dollars," DeCampo said.

Mofass started to wheeze.

I imagined Edna and Regina playing in the grass with the swans stroking them. I even worried for a moment that a swan might hurt my baby girl.

"So you want me to give you three-quarters of what I own?"

"That's one way of looking at it." DeCampo shrugged. "But a better way is to say that we are going increase your current wealth twentyfold."

The room was pretty quiet for a while. The only sound was Mofass' harsh breath.

I once thought that businessmen had some kind of honor or code. But I was straightened out about that long before I met Mr. DeCampo and his friends. I knew that there was something shady going on, and I had Mofass set up that meeting to find out exactly what it was. The next step I'd planned would give us a little time to look into their claims.

Mofass cleared his throat.

"Well, gentlemen," he said as we both rose. "I will have to discuss this with my board."

"What?" Mr. Vie asked.

"I represent a syndicate of my own, sir. Mr. Rawlins here owns a small part of that organization, and there are others. Businessmen down in our own community."

"But you led us to believe that you owned that property?" Fargo's question sounded more like a threat.

"I'm sorry if I misrepresented myself. You see, my partners like their privacy too."

"How soon will you have an answer, Mr. Wharton?" DeCampo asked, though his mouth didn't seem to move.

"Two days at the outside. I might know by this afternoon."

With that Mofass and I went to the door.

DeCampo followed us there. He shook my hand and beamed his cold smile into my eyes. Then he took Mofass' hand and held on to it.

"This information is to be held in confidence, Mr. Wharton. Nobody who doesn't need to know should be told."

I made it out of the door without having said a word.

/EVENTEEN

WE WERE DRIVING down Venice Boulevard, heading back toward Watts. The trolley had already been shut down but the tracks still ran down the center of the street. Everybody had to have a car without the trolley running.

They were drinking champagne in Detroit.

"What do you want me to tell them, Mr. Rawlins?"

"When he calls ya tell'im that we'll take a forty-sixty deal. We get the sixty."

"An' what if he don't buy that?"

"Then he's fucked. We go to Bank of America and lay it out to them the way DeCampo laid it out to us."

"I don't know," Mofass said tentatively.

"You don't know what?"

"A million dollars is a lotta money. My broker's fee of nine percent look pretty good. Why you wanna shake that up?"

"If they could give me one million, then they could make three. If they can do that then I could do it."

"I guess," Mofass said. But I'm not sure that he agreed with me.

For the rest of the ride we were quiet. Mofass hacked a little. I dreamed about being one of the few black millionaires in America. It was a strange kind of daydream, because whenever I thought of some Beverly Hills shopkeeper smiling at me I also thought that he was lying, that he really hated me. Even in my dreams I was persecuted by race.

When we were back in the office I asked, "How much money we got in the floor?"

"Nine hunnert eighty-seven."

"Gimme it."

Ordinarily Mofass would have questioned me on that hefty withdrawal but after talking six and seven figures he didn't bat an eye.

He lifted the carpet that lay before the desk. Under that was a plain pine floor. But if you slid a screwdriver between two of the boards you could pop out the small trapdoor. Down there is where we kept a certain percentage of cash receipts. That was our expense money.

Mofass pulled out the cash box and handed me what folding money there was.

When I was halfway down the stairs Mofass' phone rang. I figured it was Jack DeCampo checking to see if Mofass had an answer yet.

"Hey, baby!" I said out of the car window.

Regina looked trim and neat in her orange-and-white dress.

She was standing in front of Temple. It was five o'clock exactly.

She didn't smile, just ran across the street and jumped in. We both leaned into an awkward kiss and said hello.

Her mood was nervous, jumpy.

"What's wrong?" I asked.

"It's just that I been workin, all day an' I wanna get away from here now."

So I pulled away from the curb and turned back toward home.

"Did you find that boy?" she asked me.

"Yeah."

"Did he know who the killer was?"

"Maybe he knew somethin', but we got to see yet. All he saw was a big man with a beard. Then all he saw was stars."

"You tell Quinten Naylor that?"

"Sure did," I said. Then, "Hey, honey, I'll tell you what. Why don't you tell Gabby Lee t'stay a couple'a days with Edna and Jesus?"

"Why?"

"Then we could go up to Frisco for two nights."

"Uh . . . not tomorrow, baby," she said, looking for other words. "I can't right now."

"Is it 'cause you want that money for your auntie?"

"No, it ain't that. I got a letter from my Uncle Andrew. He said that her husband came up with what they needed anyway."

"Then what is it?"

"Do you love me, Easy?"

I felt the afternoon sun burning on my face. It was like a red-hot slap that lingers long after you've been hit.

"Sure . . . I mean, yeah, of course I do."

"Maybe you don't. Maybe you just think you do."

"Don't do this, Regina. Don't play with me."

"I ain't playin' with you. It's just a feelin' I got, that's all."

"What feeling'?" I was sitting down but I might just as well have been on my knees.

"You don't talk to me. I mean, you don't say nuthin'."

"What am I doin' right now? Ain't this talk?"

"What's my auntie's name?"

"What?"

"You know that today is the first time you ever asked me to do anything for you, Easy? You never talk to me about what you be doin'. I mean, you say you work for Mofass but I don't have no idea where you are most the time."

"So now I gotta sign in with you?"

"You was readin' a book the other day," she said, ignoring my question.

"Yeah . . ."

"I don't know what it was. I don't know what your mother's name was or who your friends are, not really."

"You don't wanna know them," I said. I laughed a little and shook my head.

"But I do wanna know. How can you know a man if you don't know his friends?"

"They ain't really friends, Gina. They more like business partners," I said. "I ain't got what you call any real friends left. My mother is dead and there ain't no more to say about that."

I turned on Ninety-sixth Street and parked. ". . . and I love you."

I don't know how I expected her to take that. She sat as far away from me as she could, with her back against the door. She shook her fine head and said, "I know you feel about me, but I don't know if it's love."

"What's that supposed to mean?"

"Sometimes you look at me the same way a dog be lookin'

after raw meat. I get scared'a the way you look at me, scared'a what you might do."

"Like what?"

"Like the other night."

I didn't know what to say then. I thought about what she called rape. I didn't think that it was like some of these men do to women, how they grab them off the street and brutalize them. But I knew that if she was unwilling then I made her against that will. I was wrong but I didn't have the heart to admit it.

My silence infuriated her.

"Do you wanna fuck me right here?" she spat.

"Com'on, baby. Don't talk like that."

"Oh? I ain't s'posed t'say it? I'm just s'posed to shut my mouf while you fuck me raw?"

"I'm sorry."

"What?"

"I'm sorry."

"You sorry? Is that what you have to say? You want to apologize for raping me?"

I was facing her. I flung backward with my elbow and shattered the glass in the door. There was a sharp pain in my upper arm; I was glad for the distraction.

"What the hell you think you doin', Easy?" Regina screamed. There was fear in her voice.

"We gotta slow this down, Gina. We gotta stop before we go someplace we cain't get down from." My voice was small and careful.

I started the car and drove off again. She gazed ahead. I looked out too, looked out for anything that would take my mind away from the anger in that car.

The thing I struck on was the palm trees. Their silhouettes rose above the landscape like impossibly tall and skinny girls.

Their hair a mess, their posture stooped. I tried to imagine what they might be thinking but failed.

"You gotta talk to me," Regina said. "You gotta hear me too."

"What do you want me to say?"

She looked out the window but I don't think she was seeing anything. "I raised thirteen hungry brothers and served my father eggs to go with his whiskey in the morning."

"I know that."

"NO YOU DON'T!"

I'd never heard her shout like that.

"I said, no you don't," Regina said again. I could hear the breath ripping from her nostrils. "I mean, you know it happened but you don't know what it is to have fourteen men leanin' on you and cryin' to you. Beggin' you all the time for everything, everything you got. Your last nickel, your Saturday night. An' they never once asked about me. They come in hungry or beat up or drunk and needin' me t'make it right."

I pulled up in front of our house. When I moved my left arm to open the door there came the sound of broken glass settling.

"But they was better than you," Regina said. "At least they needed me for somethin'. I mean, maybe you want some pussy. Maybe you even wanna make me crazy and make me come. But if I do that and fall in love with you, all you gonna do is walk outta the house in the mornin' goin' who knows where."

"Everybody goes to work, baby."

"You don't understand. I want to be part of something. I ain't just some girl to suck your dick an' have your babies."

When Marla talked like that I got excited. But hearing it from my wife made me want to tear off her head. I held my temper, though. I knew I deserved her abuse.

She stared dead ahead and I kept silent, watching the clock on the dashboard. After four minutes had gone by I said, "I got that money if you need it."

"I don't want it."

"I'll bring you down to the places I work at and show you what I do."

"Yeah . . ." she said, waiting for more.

"We could throw a party and invite the people I know."

She turned fifteen degrees and softened just a little. It was then that I caught the scent of fried okra. They had served fried okra at the wake for my mother. I was barely seven years old and I hated the minister's eyes.

I hadn't eaten friend okra in twenty-nine years, but I smelled it sometimes. Usually when I was feeling strong emotions about a woman who was almost within my reach, just beyond touch.

"I do love you, Easy." It hurt her to say it.

The glass fell out onto the ground when I got out of the car. I had to brush the shards away in order to close the door again.

"You're bleeding," Regina said.

The blood had run down my arm, making a red seam all the way down to the tip of my baby finger.

Gabby was watching the evening news from the couch and Edna was examining the frills of a small pillow under the big woman's head.

"Give us a minute, Lee," Regina said. Then she led me to the bathroom, where she made me take off my shirt.

"There's glass in this." Her probing fingers made me jump. "Does it hurt?"

"Only when you mash on it," I whimpered.

When she cleaned out the cut the blood flowed more easily.

I watched Regina's face in the cabinet mirror as she wrapped the bandage around my upper arm. The pain was welcome. So was her touching me.

We made dinner together and played with the children. Jesus showed us his quizzes. A D in spelling but an A in math. Edna tore back and forth across the floor and screeched. Nobody talked much.

At about nine o'clock the phone rang.

"Hello?"

"Is this Mr. Rawlins?"

"Who's this?" I answered.

"My name is Vernor Garnett. You nearly gave my wife a heart attack today."

"How did you get this number, Mr. Garnett?"

"I work downtown, Rawlins. I can get just about anything I want."

"Okay, sir. Maybe I shouldn't have been so hard on your wife. But I've been working with the police on this thing and I felt I needed to find out some things."

"The police say that you were to be helping them with problems in the colored community. You had no business at my house."

"Your daughter was in my community, Mr. Garnett. She worked down here."

"You leave my family alone, Rawlins. You keep out of my life. Do you understand that?"

"Yessir. Right away, sir."

I cradled the phone and it started ringing in my hand. It was too fast to be Garnett calling back so I was civil.

"Yes?"

"What's wrong with you, Rawlins?"

"Who is this?" I asked for the second time in as many minutes.

"This is Horace Voss. Who gave you permission to go into
that family's house and to leave evidence with them?"

"I guess you don't wanna work wit' me, right?"

"I want you out of this thing completely. All the way out!"

I hung up the phone again. Then I left it off the hook until
about eleven, when we went to bed.

I got up at one to change the bandage. It was too tight, but I
didn't want Regina to feel that I didn't appreciate her work.

I bathed the cut in witch hazel and wrapped it loosely with
gauze and tape. I was just finishing up when the telephone rang.

It only rang once.

Regina was waiting for me in the hall.

"One'a your girlfriends," she informed me.

I followed her back into the bedroom and picked the receiver
up off my pillow.

"Hello?"

"Thank God it's you, Easy. They got Raymond in jail."

"Who is this?" I asked for the third time.

"Minnie Fry."

That was Raymond "Mouse" Alexander's most-the-time
girlfriend.

"Okay, Minnie. Now calm down. Who got Mouse?"

"The po-lice do!"

"Is he dead?"

"They holdin' him. He want me to call you first off."

"Down here at the Seventy-seventh?"

"Um-huh. You gotta go down there right now."

"It's almost two . . ."

"You gotta go right now, Easy! That's what Raymond said."

Mouse had faced loaded guns for me more than once. He had been my friend since we were young men, and even though Raymond was always close to mayhem, I knew he was the closest to family that I had outside of my wife and kids.

"All right," I sighed. "I'll go down there."

"You gonna go right now?" Minnie asked.

"I said all right, didn't I?"

"Okay. But you gotta go now."

We went back and forth like that three or four times before I could get her off the phone.

I got my clothes from the closet.

"My dressing wasn't good enough for you?" Regina asked as I put on my pants.

"A little tight is all. I just changed it."

"Where you goin' now?"

"Down to the police station."

"You gonna get drunk and fuck that girl down there?"

"That was Minnie Fry on the phone, babe. That's Mouse's girl. She said that Mouse was in jail."

"What's that got to do with you?"

"He's my friend, Regina. An' I could get him out."

"You cain't wait till mornin'?"

"He wouldn't wait for me."

Regina sucked her tooth and went back to bed. I leaned over her, to kiss her before I left, but she wasn't interested.

EIGHTEEN

THE NIGHT SERGEANT didn't believe that I worked for Quinten Naylor. But he didn't mind making an early-morning call to his superior officer either. So I waited while he tried to get through.

It was a quiet night at the station.

An old man nodded in and out of sleep on the long wooden bench where we both sat. He was a white wino, not uncommon in our neighborhood. His coat had once been brown but now it was worn to gray at places. He smelled of sweat and that made me like him. Across from us sat a middle-aged black woman. She was weeping into a blue handkerchief. Her cheeks and nose were bright black plums. I never knew why either one of them was there. I've spent my whole life passing by little tragedies like that and ignoring them.

"Mr. Rawlins," the desk sergeant called.

"Yeah?"

"Lieutenant Naylor said to let you see the man. Just fill this out and I'll get somebody to bring you back." He held out a clipboard with a mimeographed sheet of paper on it.

I put down my name and address and relationship with the incarcerated. I put down my social security number and my telephone number and the reason for my visit. I signed at the bottom and returned the clipboard to the sergeant.

He didn't even read it, just folded the page into quarters and pushed it down a slot behind him. Then he picked up the phone and pushed a button on the desk.

"Come on out here, Rivers," was all he said into the receiver.

A moment later a small white man in a short-sleeved khaki police shirt came out of a door behind the sergeant's desk. The man had a gaunt and pitted face. He was probably in his mid-thirties but he could have been sixty with a ravaged face like that.

"This the guy?"

The sergeant nodded.

"Come on," the ravaged man said. "I'm in a goddamned rush."

First he took me down a long gray-plaster hall. We came to a white wooden door that the policeman had a key for. Just beyond that door was another one, an iron door with evil-looking bolts all around it. He had a key for this door too. Then we were in another hall made of steel-grated floors, walls, and ceilings.

We came to a big room made all out of metal and glass. There was a table in the middle of the floor with a chair on either side. The table and chairs were all bolted to the floor.

I heard the gruff voice of one man talking and the pathetic sobs of another man.

"Sit down. Wait here," the little policeman said. Then he went through a door on the other side.

"I ain't tellin' you again!" It was the gruff voice.

In answer a man moaned. Then there was a loud crash and more crying. I heard the voice again but I couldn't make out what was being said.

The noise was coming from behind an iron door to my right.

The door behind me opened and Mouse, manacled hand and foot, shuffled in, followed by the warder.

It made me sick at heart to see Raymond like that. He was the only black man I'd ever known who had never been chained, in his mind, by the white man. Mouse was brash and wild and free. He might have been insane, but any Negro who dared to believe in his own freedom in America had to be mad. The sight of his incarceration made me shudder inside.

Rivers pushed Mouse toward the chair. Once Raymond was seated the policeman padlocked his chains through two metal loops in the floor. Then he went to sit in a stool in the corner, giving us as little privacy as he could.

I could still hear the arguing, moaning, and fighting from behind the iron door, but the guard and Mouse seemed unconcerned.

"You got a piece, Easy?" he whispered.

"What?"

"You got a gun?"

"No, no. I ain't comin' in no jail with a gun."

"I need to get out of here," Mouse said slowly. "They want to change my address to Folsom Prison an' that ain't gonna happen."

"Why they got you in here, Raymond?"

"They wanna frame me on them killin's. They need somebody t'hang."

"Why you?"

"I don't know, man. They say I knowed a couple'a them girls. Maybe I did, you know I always be after that stuff. But that don't mean I kilt no girls."

"So you didn't do it?"

"Do what?"

"What they said, man. Kill them girls."

"What? You think I'm crazy?"

Yes, I thought. Crazy and a killer in everything he did. He was a slight man, not over five-seven, with gold-edged teeth and a pencil-thin mustache. The police hadn't issued him jail clothes. He was decked out in green suede shoes, drab green pants, and a loose bright pink shirt that flopped around his wrists because they had taken his cufflinks.

He'd murdered his stepfather for a wedding dowry. He would have lied to God with his final breath.

"I just wanna know why they pulled you in here," I said. "That's all."

"Please, no," came a cry from behind the iron door.

I looked around at the guard but he was reading a paperback western.

"It don't matter why I'm here, Easy," Mouse said. "What matters is that you get me out."

Every now and then there was a dull thud against the iron door.

"Gimme a few hours," I said.

When the little guard led me back out of that hell I could have almost kissed the floor.

I was reading the morning paper at the sergeant's desk when Quinten Naylor arrived. It was seven-sixteen in the morning.

He motioned me to follow him and we both walked back to his office.

We sat with our coffee and cigarettes. Quinten nodded and asked, "What can I do for you?"

"Why you got Mouse down here, man?"

"Mr. Alexander is suspected of having information about a homicide." His face was wooden.

"You ain't got a damn thing on him."

"Do you know who did the killings?"

"What about that bearded guy I told you 'bout? He coulda done it."

"No corroboration. The owners of Aretha's denied the story."

"What about Gregory Jewel?"

"He says that he never saw the man that hit him."

"And you believe that?"

"Do you have something for me, Rawlins? Because if you don't I have business to take care of." He motioned his head toward the door, then he picked up a pencil and started writing on a white legal pad.

"What about Mouse?"

"He stays in jail until we have something better."

"On what charges?"

Naylor put down his pencil and looked at me. "No charge. He stays here two more days, then he gets transferred to the Hollywood station. After that we send him downtown. We could keep him tied up for months and even the commissioner wouldn't be able to find him."

"You proud'a that?"

"Are you going to find our killer?"

"I thought Voss wanted me out."

"He's not the only one involved. Violette wants you in. He's willing to kill your friend to make sure of it."

"Let Mouse out," I said.

"No can do."

"Let'im out an' we'll find this killer together. I'ma need a helper if this thing gets full-time with me."

"He's a prime suspect, Easy. He's been everywhere those girls were. Even your Cyndi Starr."

"I don't think he did it."

"How would you know?"

"Raymond wouldn't kill those girls like that. But if you leave him in jail people gonna die for sure. Anyway, he told me he didn't have nuthin' t'do with it. He ain't got no reason t'lie t'me. Gimme a week with Raymond and we'll turn up what you need."

Quinten shook his head. "I don't know."

"Call Violette. Ask him," I said. "I'll be out at the bench when you get an answer."

I waited an hour and fifteen minutes for Naylor to come out. He had Mouse with him. Mouse was fastening his cufflinks and smiling at me. It was a killer's smile that reminded all the ladies of a sweet loving child.

NINETEEN

MOUSE WAS LIVING with Minnie Fry at that time. They had a one-room cottage on Vernon.

She was sleeping in the Murphy bed when we got there.

"Hey, Minnie! Yo' boy is home," Mouse called as we came crashing into the room.

The only thing I could see of Minnie was her head. The rest of her was just a lump under a thick pink quilt. But when Mouse announced himself she yelled (I swear), "Oh boy!" and threw the bedding aside. All she wore was a tiny pair of pink panties but she didn't mind my eyes. She ran up to Mouse and hugged him to her large bosom as if he were the Lord called up from the dead.

"Baby!" she cried. She kissed him and hugged him some more. "Baby!"

Minnie was a head taller and fifty pounds heavier than

Mouse. She swung him from side to side until he stopped holding on to her and started trying to push away.

"Stop it, Minnie. Stop it fo' you send me to the hospital."

She just kept crooning and swaying. I don't think anybody ever missed me as much as that woman missed him. I was away from home for years in World War II and nobody waited at the shore to hold me like that.

"Put me down, girl," Mouse pleaded. I could see that he was smiling, though. "Go get decent fo' you shame ole Easy here."

Minnie didn't mind showing off her generous black figure as long as we didn't mention it, but when he said that she folded her arms around her chest and ducked a little as she scooped some clothes from a chair. She held these in front of her and tiptoed into the bathroom.

Mouse smiled after her. "She sumpin', huh, Easy?"

Minnie was out of the bathroom in two minutes. She wore a plain blue dress that she'd probably sewn from a pattern in home economics when she was still in high school. You could see the uneven seams along the blue straps that covered her shoulder. The dress was a little snug, because she'd gained a few pounds in the two years since she'd gotten her diploma.

"Place is a pigsty," Mouse said, curling his lip with distaste. "I only been in jail one day. How could you do all this?"

Minnie just wilted.

Mouse held out his hands in a helpless gesture. "What's that you say?"

"I didn't say nuthin', baby."

"Then what do you have to say? I mean, I come home to a hog barn an' you just gonna wave yo' titties in Easy's face?"

I felt for Minnie's shame but there was nothing I could do to help her. What Mouse wanted to say was that we were going to have to talk business so we were going out again. But he couldn't say something straight forward like that, so he criticized her cleaning in order that he could excuse himself while she got the house together.

"Now we gonna start over," Mouse said. "I'ma go with Easy now an' get some breakfast . . ."

"I'll cook for ya, baby," Minnie interrupted.

"Uh-uh, no. We gonna go down to the Pie Pan an' get us some food, and when we get back the house and you is gonna be just fine. Ain't that right?"

"Uh-huh. But I could get cleaned up real quick, Raymond . . ."

Mouse shook his head and frowned. "I don't wanna hear it, Minnie. We goin' now."

We did go to the Pie Pan. Mouse had toast, jelly, and hot chocolate. I ordered grits, sausages, and eggs scrambled with cubed potatoes and onions. We didn't talk at first because Mouse's hands were shaking. Over the years I had learned that as long as Mouse's hands were still shaking he could kill over the smallest slight. When he got nervous, violence was his easiest and first outlet. That's why I didn't take Minnie's part in the house. He might have struck her, or me, if he felt that his will was being questioned.

So we ate and smoked and waited for the jailhouse shakes to subside.

After the meal was over and we were both drinking tea with lemon I said, "We gotta find the man did them killin's, Raymond."

"All right wit' me. You know I wanna kill me some mothahfuckah. I don't take to no cell."

"We can't kill'im, Raymond. I want the law off both of us an' the only way we could do that is t'give'em somebody t'hang."

"I might not have t'kill'im, but you know I might shoot'im a li'l just the same. S'pose he a big boy don't respect my pistol?"

I didn't argue. If Mouse wanted to hurt somebody there was no way to stop him. I had to accept his insane violence if I wanted his help.

I told him everything that I'd learned. I told him about Aretha's and the whorehouse. I told him about Gregory Jewel and Cyndi Starr. In forty-five minutes he knew everything I did.

"What this white girl gotta do with it?"

"Bad luck, I guess."

"Bad luck my ass."

"What you mean?"

"I don't know, Easy. But we gonna find out. Who we gonna talk to first? You wanna try them boys who beat up on you?"

"Not right now. They were just hands. Probably come after me 'cause Max thought it would keep me off them. It's just bad for business have somebody 'round talkin' 'bout killin'."

"Gregory Jewel?"

"Uh-uh. He don't know nuthin'. No. It's Charlene Mars and Westley we talk to. Charlene told the cops that she never saw no man go up against Gregory Jewel. I don't know why, she could just be lyin' to fuck with 'em, but I think she knows somethin' too. Otherwise she'd tell 'em the little bit she knew."

"Sound good to me. You wanna go over there now?"

"Uh-uh. Tonight, after they close."

Mouse's eyes lit up. "I'll meet ya out front at two."

I nodded and shook his hand. Then I took him over to Minnie's house so he could spend the afternoon making up to her.

When I got home there was a note waiting from Jesus' gym teacher.

Jesus had gotten into a fight with two boys who were taunting him. When the gym teacher tried to stop them Jesus hit him in the nose.

"Don't be too hard on'im, Easy," Regina said after I'd read the note. "You know children always be ridin' a child who's different."

"He gotta learn to keep his anger in check," I answered. I was always happy that Regina cared about Jesus. She just accepted him.

I might have sounded tough to her but I wasn't very upset by Jesus' crime.

Still, I put on a severe face and went into the boy's room. But when I saw him, curled up behind his knees on the bed, I knew that he'd already learned more than I could bully him into.

He shuddered when I sat next to him. I patted his shoulder and smiled as softly as I could.

"Don't worry, boy," I said. "We gonna go straighten this out in the morning."

Jesus looked at me with frightened eyes. He nodded as if to say, "Really?"

"Yeah. I know you a good boy, Jesus. You wouldn't fight unless you thought you had to. But I want you to promise me that you won't never fight unless somebody hits you or tries to hit you."

His gaze gained confidence. He smiled and nodded.

" 'Cause you know a man can control you if he can drive you to fight over some shit he talks."

Jesus nodded again.

Jesus put his cold hands on my neck and kissed me just off to the left of my nose. When he hugged me I was amazed at how hot his cheek was.

"Let's go get some dinner now," I said.

At dinner Regina and I sat across the table avoiding eye contact like strangers who are uncertain about striking up a conversation.

When the baby and Jesus were asleep I brought a thick envelope with nine hundred dollars in it to her.

"Here's all the money you wanted and then some," I said.

She looked at me with clear serious eyes. I waited for her to say something but the words never came. Instead her face softened and she pulled me down in the bed, on top of her.

We didn't make love, just lay there like spoons with me holding her from behind. At one o'clock I moved away and dressed. I looked back at her from the door as I left. Her eyes were open wide, taking me in. I put my finger in front of my lips and waved. She just stared after me. God knows what she was thinking.

TWENTY

I PARKED DOWN the block from Aretha's. Bone Street's denizens staggered alone and in pairs. There was shouting and kissing and vomiting on the sidewalk. The last ones to leave Aretha's were the strippers. Big women on the whole who trudged toward their homes like tired soldiers returning from the front lines.

It was two-twenty when I looked at my watch but that didn't bother me. I knew Mouse would be there when I needed him. He would always be there in my life, smiling and ready to commit mayhem.

The door to Aretha's hadn't opened in a while when he strolled out. He was wearing a bright yellow double-breasted jacket and dark brown pants. His silk shirt was blue and stamped all over with bright orange triangles. His close-cropped head was hatless. I guess Mouse figured that a man dressed like that just couldn't be killed.

He walked up to my window and said, "It's only them two now, Easy. I'da gotten what you wanted myself but I didn't wanna cheat you outta the fun."

"Door open?" I asked.

"Naw. They locked up when I left but I put a wedge on the back do'. We could go in when you want to."

We cut down the alley that ran parallel to Bone and through a little gate that led to the back door of the bar. Mouse straight-handed the door, pushing it open into a large dark room. Then we went through a doorway that came to another door. This door was edged in light. I could hear Charlene and Westley talking on the other side.

Mouse was the first one through. I heard Charlene gasp and Westley say, "What?" and then I came in.

They were seated at a small round table in front of the stage. Both of them staring at both of us. There was an electricity in the air. Westley looked like he wanted to make a break for the door.

If Charlene was going to break something it would be our heads. "What are you doin' in here?" It was more of a warning than a question.

"Easy got sumpin' t'ask," Mouse said in his friendliest tone.

"Get the hell outta here," Charlene said, but then she froze. I looked over and saw that Mouse had drawn his pistol.

"I ain't here t'play, Charlene. We need t'know what we need t'know an' you is gonna tell us," Mouse said.

"What you want from us?" Westley asked. His eyes were moving from side to side in a shifty manner. I knew that he was up to something and that scared me. I wasn't worried about him hurting us or getting away. What worried me was that Mouse might kill poor Westley and then I'd be struggling to get *myself* out of jail.

"Tell me 'bout the fight with that man and Gregory Jewel," I said quickly. Maybe we'd get what we wanted and get out before things got out of hand.

"I told you what I know already, Easy Rawlins." That was Charlene. "And then you go tryin' to get me in bad with the police."

"I wanna know who that man was, Charlene. Either you tell me or you convince me that you don't know."

"And what if I don't?" the big woman dared.

Mouse's grin was a boy's joy on a hot summer's day. Westley brought his foot up to his seat and put his hands together at the ankle. He had on red socks but I caught a glimpse of brown leather too. Westley pulled a small pistol from his pant leg. I yelled, "No!" and shoved my hand against Mouse's gun-bearing arm. Charlene called, "Oh no." The shots, big and small, deafened me. I saw Westley pitch sideways out of his chair.

Charlene cried, "West!" and ran to his side.

Mouse swung the barrel of his pistol at my head but I stepped out of the way. "What the fuck is wrong with you, Easy?" he cried.

I knew better than to answer. Mouse glared at me while Charlene was desperate over Westley. There was blood oozing down the bartender's arm.

Mouse went up to them and pushed Charlene aside. He checked the bartender's wound and moved away again taking the bartender's pistol with him.

"He ain't gonna die," Mouse said.

"Tell me," I said to Charlene.

Mouse clacked back the hammer of his pistol.

"His name is Saunders," she said in even, defeated tones. "He's bad news from here to St. Louis. Get inta fights and use his knife. I didn't want no trouble with him."

"Even if he was killin' girls?" I asked.

"I didn't know nuthin' 'bout no killin's. I see men and women do what he did to Gregory Jewel almost every night."

I remembered how Jasper Filagret was beaten over Dorthea.

"He got any friends?" I asked.

"One time he brought this cousin'a his down here. Red-headed man he called Abernathy. He works at Federal Butcher's with my nephew, Tiny. That's all I know."

Mouse turned friendly then. He got a rag from behind the bar and handed it to Charlene.

"He only got it in the shoulder," Mouse said. "He lucky Easy hit me."

Outside Mouse wasn't smiling. "Don't you never do that again, Easy Rawlins."

"You might have killed him."

"Westley coulda got us both if I didn't get him in the arm. Next time I shoot you too."

He wasn't lying.

With that over, Mouse's anger faded away. "We gotta take this butcher boy first thing, Easy. We could lay for him 'fore he even go into work."

"I can't till later."

"How come?"

"I gotta go to school with Jesus in the mornin'. He got trouble with some teacher and I have to go with him." All of a sudden I was very tired. I almost dozed off while we spoke.

"All right. Why don't you come on around Minnie's after that?"

I agreed. We said our goodbyes, then I drove home. I parked

in front of my house but didn't have the strength to open the door.

I was thinking about a dead woman sitting peacefully under a tree. Mouse was talking to her. Talking and talking. Whatever he was saying he read from a little black book, like a telephone diary.

She just sat there, peacefully listening. Mouse went on talking. A thousand birds gathered in the trees. They were waiting silently for Mouse to finish talking so they could descend on the corpse and pluck the flesh from her bones.

TWENTY ONE

I HEARD LOUD snoring and wondered that I had never heard Regina snore like that before. I lifted my hand to nudge her and touched something that was hard and smooth, the steering wheel. It was my own breathing that I heard. I stared up out of the windshield at the overcast skies. Even that dim light hurt my eyes.

It took many minutes for me to sit up.

Breathing slowly and taking small steps, I made it to the house. Regina was still asleep. It was five A.M. I stayed in the bathtub until I heard her moving around. Then I shaved and toweled off.

I was in the kitchen drinking coffee when she came in. She wore a flowered housecoat that had a bright orange-and-blue painting of a macaw down the left side.

"You didn't come home last night," she said.

I felt like a man who'd walked off the street and into a play. Nobody would let me off the stage until I said my lines, but I'd forgotten them.

Regina got a mugful of coffee and sat across from me. "Well?"

"The cops need me to find a toehold. They put Mouse in jail so I'd tell'em I'd do it."

She just stared.

"I went to Aretha's with Mouse last night . . ."

"Who?"

"It's a bar."

"Where?"

"On Bone Street." I tried to keep my voice normal but it lowered when I named that name.

"Oh." She nodded and her beautiful eyes closed, shutting me out for the moment.

"It ain't like that, baby. We had to get somebody to talk to us. There was a fight, it got pretty bad. I made it home but I passed out in the car. You don't have to believe me, baby. I know you might wonder at how crazy I'm actin'. But I swear it's gonna get better. I swear it."

She put the coffee mug down and got up slowly. I sat there looking up at her.

"You don't have to swear to me, Easy," she said. "I ain't yo' keeper."

"But you know it's been kinda hard on me lately."

"Don't worry. Ain't nuthin' gonna happen if you miss one night at home. That ain't gonna bother me. All I wanna know is what happened. Maybe you in love with somebody else. I just asked."

"I love you."

She picked up the mug and went into the kitchen to fix Jesus' lunch. Later Jesus came out and sat by the front door.

Regina brought him his sack. She knelt down in front of him and straightened his shirt. She ran a finger along his cheek and he smiled; more from love than the tickle he felt. When she stood up and turned I saw that there were tears in Regina's eyes.

Regina went into our room and dressed quickly. She left the house without saying goodbye. Gabby Lee came and took Edna away.

I drove up to the Eighty-ninth Street school with Jesus. It was one big blue stucco building. Three floors of classrooms and a big asphalt field behind that. To the left of the field was a small bungalow where the children would go at various times during the week for an hour of calisthenics. They'd do jumping jacks and sit-ups and running in place. I knew because I had asked Jesus what he did in each of his subjects. He showed me in books for most things but when it came to PE he did the exercises to entertain both me and Edna.

Mr. Arnet, the coach, was standing in front of a group of little boys that were lying on their backs with their hands behind their heads. They were struggling to pull themselves up by their necks.

"One, two," Mr. Arnet said. "One, two."

I don't know what he was counting. The little heads and young bellies just strained and strained.

When Mr. Arnet saw Jesus and me he said in a loud voice, "All right, everybody, elimination ball in the big square."

The children all jumped up and started screaming. Arnet pulled a white volleyball out of a canvas bag behind him and threw it into a tall boy's waiting arms. All the children went into a large white square and started throwing the ball at each other. It looked like fun.

"Mr. Rawlins?" It was Arnet. He was a tall white man with strawlike blond hair, an extremely long neck, and a potbelly. When he walked up to me I saw that he wasn't nearly my height, but the long neck made him seem tall from the distance.

"Mr. Arnet," I said. "Looks like we had a little problem."

He ran his hand back through the straw, shook his head, and gave me a rueful grin.

"I had to bend over the sink for fifteen minutes with the bloody nose your boy gave me, Rawlins."

The way he used my name, the way he said it, rubbed me wrong. I took a deep breath and tried to overcome my anger.

"He's real sorry about that, Mr. Arnet. He feels bad and I told him that I won't have him fighting like that."

The gym teacher shook his head again and shoved his hands in his pockets. He clucked his tongue, giving the impression that I had failed the test.

"Is Jesus your natural son?" he asked.

I turned to Jesus, who had been looking up at us with a scowl of concentration. "Go on to your class now, honey," I said. "Me and Mr. Arnet gonna talk a little more."

He smiled quickly and ran off toward the big blue building.

"He's a beautiful boy," I said.

"Is he yours?" Mr. Arnet asked again.

That white man's eyes were mostly yellow but clotted with little gray dots which made them seem green. They were small, cagey eyes.

"Yes," I said. "He's my boy."

"Your wife a Mexican?"

I knew what was coming. Jesus had been with me for years but he wasn't my natural son. He was a poor soul that had been kidnapped to satisfy a rich man's evil appetites. I had saved Jesus from all that and, finally, I had taken him as my son. Mr. Arnet wanted to cause trouble about that. Maybe it was because he was humiliated by Jesus or maybe it was because he had a bleeding heart.

"Do you like your job, Mr. Arnet?" I asked.

The question caught him a little off guard. He said, "What?"

"I just ask because I know that a man who feels strongly about his work will stand up and be counted no matter what. I mean, take me and Jesus. He's my boy. I love him. It was a hard thing for me to get here this morning because I'm a working man and I had to stay late on the job last night. But you know I got my ass outta bed to come here and see what's what. I love Jesus. If a man or anybody wanted to hurt him I don't know what I might do."

I looked Mr. Arnet in the eye, then I shook my head. "No. No, that's not right. If somebody fucked with my boy I would kill the bastard. Because you see I'm committed to him. I love him. He's my son."

The coach had blanched a little while I spoke. When I finished he swallowed to lubricate his vocal cords, knowing that his next words were important ones.

"I understand you, Mr. Rawlins," he said. "It's a rare parent nowadays who takes such a deep concern with their children's welfare. I'm sure Jesus will be fine now."

"You call me if he isn't," I said. "I want Jesus to grow up right."

I looked him in the eye for a moment more. He got fidgety, clasping his hands together.

"Well, it was good to meet you, Mr. Rawlins." He held his hand out. I shook it. "I've got to get back to the kids now."

He pulled a police whistle out of his pocket and blew it at the kids. Then he yelled, "All right! Line up!" and was off running toward the large white square.

I stalked out of that schoolyard with my head throbbing and my heart going fast. It seemed like everything had to happen the hard way.

I called Quinten Naylor from a phone booth. I told him that the guy who beat Gregory Jewel and went off with Juliette LeRoi was called Saunders.

By the time I got home there was a message with Gabby Lee that fifteen thousand dollars had been offered for information leading to the capture of the killer and that a bearded man named Saunders was the prime suspect.

TWENTY TWO

I WENT TO meet Mouse at eleven-fifteen. Minnie was at the beauty shop where she worked but there was another woman there. Maxine Cone, Mouse's other girlfriend.

They were sitting on the bed drinking beers when I got there. Mouse offered me one and I took it.

I was halfway through the third beer when Mouse said, "Our boy be leavin' for lunch soon."

I put the bottle down on the floor and got up.

"Where you all going?" Maxine asked. She was very dark and slight with shoulder-length coarse hair that was combed straight back and down.

"We got work to do, Maxie. You go on home an' I call later on," Mouse told her.

I thought we were going to have another fight right there. I could see Maxine's jaw clenching and her eyes narrow like gun turrets. But she kept quiet. As a matter of fact she hardly said another word. She got a sweater from a nail on the wall and walked out before us.

Mouse and I went to my car and I called to Maxine, "Could I give you a ride somewhere?"

She just walked on down the sidewalk ignoring us both. I don't think she ever talked to Mouse again. In four months she was married to Billy Tyler.

Mouse ran through women like a boy going through toys on Christmas morning. The whole year was Christmas for Mouse; his whole life was.

Federal Butcher's was in a building that I frequented in the late forties. It was a butchers' warehouse mainly, but there used to be a little bar on the third floor. Joppy's place.

Joppy had been a friend of mine for many years. He was an old friend from back in the Fifth Ward in Houston and he was a pal in L.A. when I first got there in the mid-forties. But when we did business at a bad angle Joppy ended up dead. My life had dire consequences; there were reminders of it all over Los Angeles.

Lunch hour came and went but we didn't see any redheaded black men. I went down to a package store and bought a half pint of Seagram's and two plastic cups.

By afternoon I couldn't keep my eyes open.

"Go on to sleep, Easy," Mouse said.

When the sounds of traffic got heavier and the quality of light shifted on my eyelids, I woke up. Men were coming out of the big double doors of Federal Butcher's. Some of them still wore their bloody white coats. I thought that Federal probably didn't have a laundry service and these men had to wash the blood away themselves.

"There he is," Mouse said.

A sharp-looking man in tan shirt and pants was walking quickly down Central. He had very light hair that was blond with fuzzy light-brown highlights. He was tall and well-built with an angular light brown face. He walked right past our car. Mouse started the engine and made a U-turn to follow.

When he stopped at a red light at 110th Street we parked and followed him on foot.

He went all the way to 125th Street before he turned. Then he went half the way down the block to an apartment building that was built exactly to the plans of my own Magnolia Street apartments. We waited for him to go in and then went to check the names on the mailboxes.

Randall Abernathy lived on the top floor in apartment 3C.

"Go on home, Raymond," I said.

"What?"

"I wanna talk to this one alone."

Mouse must have had something else to do, because he didn't argue with me. I was glad he didn't. I wanted to be quiet and subtle for a change.

When I knocked on door to 3C there were footsteps across the room to the door and then a moment of silence.

"Who is it?" a careful voice asked.

"Roger Stockton," I answered in a loud, hollow voice that I used sometimes.

"I don't know any Roger."

"I'm from Star Meat Packing in Santa Clara, Mr. Abernathy.

I want to discuss a job opportunity with you."

A poor man can always use a job. He might already have a job, a good one, but he can never count on that going on forever. The boss might go crazy and fire him tomorrow. Or maybe his mother will get sick and he'll need that extra cash.

I don't know for sure that Abernathy came from poverty, but he did open that door.

I put on a smile that could have gotten me elected, if I was a white man.

"Mr. Abernathy!" I grabbed his hand and pumped it. "It's good to finally meet you face to face."

A grin stumbled at his lips and Randall tried to return my warmth. But then he frowned for a second and pulled back a bit. In that same second I saw the pewter crucifix hanging around his neck, and I smelled the alcohol of my own breath.

"I wanna get right down to it, Brother Abernathy, because I don't wanna disturb your home. I got a job opportunity for a head butcher out at Star and you're the one I think I want."

"What?"

"Could I come in a minute and go over this with you?"

I limped past him into the middle of the room. I knew the layout of the apartment because of my own building. It was an efficiency unit. One moderate-sized room with a nook for a bed, an alcove for the kitchen, and a small bathroom on the side.

I could see by the decor that Abernathy was a solitary man. He had a table with one chair and a chest of drawers. The floor was swept, never mopped, and bare.

Favoring my left leg, I went to the straight-backed chair and lowered myself delicately.

"You hurt?" Abernathy asked.

There was an open Bible on the table in front of me. Half of the verses were underlined in blue ink.

"What? Oh, you mean my leg."

Abernathy stood over me and I got ready to give him my lies.

"In a way this here war wound is why I'm here. I got more shrapnel than bone in this leg. Chinee mortar from a North Korean regular did it . . ."

Abernathy perched himself on the edge of his neatly made bed.

". . . I heard the sucker comin' and jumped for the nearest hole . . . only there was this white boy named Tooms in the way so I knocks him over and takes it in the leg."

I grimaced a little and touched the imaginary wound.

Randall asked, "And that's why you're here?"

"This Tooms boy didn't know that he was in my way. He thought that I saved him on purpose." I winked. "He thinks that he owes me his life."

"If you saved him then I guess he does owe you something," Abernathy said. He was still confused about the direction of my story but he wanted to sound like he knew what was going on.

"That's how I see it too. So when his daddy told him that he wanted him to run the family business, Eugene, that's the white boy I saved, came right to me and said that he wanted me to be his manager."

"And this business is Star Meat Packing?"

I nodded with a knowing grin on my face.

"That doesn't tell me why you here, Mr. Stockton," the butcher said.

"Well." I looked around, a little uncomfortable. "I can see that you're a religious man, brother, but I can't lie to you. I was in a bar, I can't remember the name of it but it was down on Slauson. Anyway, I met this man down there. I told him this same story I told you and he's the one give me your name. He said that you was a damn good butcher but that a Negro never has no chance if the man he works for is white. I talked to a few people about you and they all said that you was a good worker and smart about meat."

"Who was this man?"

I managed to keep the excitement out of my voice as I said, "I forget his first name but the bartender kept callin' him Mr. Saunders."

Randall couldn't have stood up faster if he'd been sitting on hot coals.

"A big man?"

"With a beard," I replied, nodding.

"When did you say this was?"

I hunched my shoulders. "I don't know. Two weeks ago, maybe three."

"Then why you gettin' to me just now?" Abernathy was mad about something.

"I told you. Eugene made me the manager out at Star. He got me workin', tryin' t'learn the trade. You know they got me studyin' saws an' scales an' how t'read the black mold on beef. I tell ya, I never knew there was so much to cuttin' a steak. What's wrong with callin' on you three weeks later?"

"It's just that I can't see Saunders braggin' about me to nobody."

"He *was* actin' kinda strange, now that you mention it. But I thought it was just how much he was drinkin'. He kept on talkin' 'bout women too."

"Women," Abernathy said as if it were a curse. "Women is what destroyed that man." His tone approached that of a minister infused with the Holy Spirit.

"He looked okay to me."

"But on the inside he's rotten. Rotting away for all the evil he's done. There's no hiding from the Lord's retribution. Without faith them sulfa drugs won't do a thing. No no. Syphilis is the Lord's punishment for fornication."

His face flushed and his lips quivered. There was some insanity in Saunders' family, that much was clear.

"Well, at least he told me about you," I said. "Why don't we talk about you coming out to Star."

I told him all about Star and how much I needed a head butcher I could trust. We set a date two weeks away for him to come out and meet Eugene Tooms. I gave him a fake number and address.

Randall was happy by the end of our talk. He was going to double his salary and get a chance to be a partner in the business.

"Where can I get in touch with your cousin?" I asked at the door.

"J.T.? Why?"

"I don't know. He was good to me. Bought me a few drinks and gave me your name. That's worth a thank-you I suppose."

"He's gone."

"Gone? Gone where?"

"Up north."

"Frisco?"

"His family lives up in Oakland. They live up there but I've never been."

Regina, Jesus, and Edna were all on the front porch. Jesus was lying across Regina's lap and Edna sat next to them playing with a pink-and-blue ball. They all looked at me as I came up the four steps.

"Hi, honey," Regina said. Her voice was happy but she didn't look me in the eye.

Edna squealed and threw the ball at me.

"Hi, everybody."

Edna tried to run off her chair but Jesus caught her and tickled her so she wouldn't cry.

"Jesus," I said. "Take Edna in the house and play horse for a while."

Jesus and Edna loved the horse game. They'd both crawl around on all fours, crashing into things. Regina never let them play it, but I would when I needed to be alone for a while.

I kissed my wife and led her by the hand to the fence at the front of the yard. Some ignorant city gardener had planted an oak in the unpaved part of the sidewalk. The tree had grown and its roots were buckling the sidewalk on one side and the street on the other. Its trunk was gnarly and dark and it was shady there.

"What can you tell me about syphilis?" I asked.

"Why?" Regina's hand stiffened and she pulled away from me.

"Not because'a me, baby," I said. "But maybe this killer has it. I heard that he had been taking sulfa drugs."

"How long has he had it?"

"I don't know really. But they say that it's pretty bad."

"If it is bad then all kindsa things could be wrong with him. VD can make you insane."

"Do they have special records of people been on these things?" I asked. "I know they had special hospitals down in Texas."

"I could find out."

"His name is Saunders, J. T. Saunders. And he was on the cure before they came up with penicillin."

We kissed lightly but then she moved away from me as we walked back to the house. Jesus and Edna had knocked over a table and there was water all over the floor.

TWENTY THREE

THE NEXT MORNING I went around checking on my various properties. I had a carpenter from Guatemala laying a floor in an apartment on Quigley Street and a gardener to talk to who hadn't mown a lawn in six weeks. I looked at the different places, picked up some trash, and noted certain infractions for Mofass to follow up.

Then I took a ride over to Mofass' office.

I found him hacking from deep in his lungs into a big yellow rag. He was coughing when I came into the room and he coughed while he told me that the DeCampo people had agreed to my demands.

"Mr. DeCampo called me himself," Mofass wheezed.

"That was mighty white of him."

I regretted saying that, because it sent Mofass into an even

more virulent bout of coughing. Coughs racked his whole frame
and tears nearly spurted from his eyes.

After long moments barking up sputum Mofass finally rasped
out a question. "You gonna sign with them?"

I was afraid to tell him the truth. I thought he would drop
dead if I refused him then.

I said, "Well, let's meet again and see what they got on
paper."

I had no intention of letting those thieves steal what was
mine. If a major road went near my property then I could deal
with a bank and keep a hundred percent of my business.

"I'm gonna use your phone," I said.

"I need to go home anyways," he said. "This cold got me by
the nuts."

I watched him put on his overcoat and hat. The weight of his
garments seemed to drag him almost to the floor. I watched him
go out the door and then I listened as his cough retreated down
the stairs.

I sat down and dialed the number that I knew best.

"Temple Hospital," a nasally white woman informed me.

"Sixth-floor maternity, please."

There was a pause and then some clicks and buzzes. Finally
another, richer voice said, "Nurse's station."

"Regina Rawlins, please."

"She's kinda busy right now. Who is it?"

"Louise," I said, "will you please go get my wife?"

"Easy?"

"How you doin', Louise? Regina said you were workin'
again."

"Fine, baby." I could hear her gap-toothed grin. "I sure do
miss you."

"You got Regina around there?"

"Mm. Too in love for a kind word?"

"With a woman as beautiful as you a man cain't take no chances, Louie."

"Okay. That's good enough."

After another wait my wife finally came on the line.

"Hi, honey," she said.

"Babe."

"He was tested in a hospital in Oxnard. It was a public hospital but affiliated with the navy. He was an able-bodied seaman in the merchant marines and they paid for his treatments.

"Does he still go there?"

"Not in a long time. His last visit was in 1938. He only went for three months. The clerk there said that he'd be really sick by now if he didn't get treatment somewhere."

"You get an address?"

"Just what he left back then. Twenty-four eighty-nine Stockard Street, Oakland, California. The phone was Axminister 2-854."

I wrote all that down on a pad that Mofass kept on his desk.

"I'll take you out for steaks if you get Gabby Lee to sit for the kids," I said.

"I can't tonight, baby." She sounded upset about it. "I spent so much time on this stuff for you that I had to promise Miss Butler that I'd stay late."

"Can't you do it tomorrow?"

"I gotta go now, honey. Good luck."

When I cradled the phone I felt very lonely. All of what I had and all I had done was had and done in secret. Nobody knew the real me. Maybe Mouse and Mofass knew something but they weren't friends that you could kick back and jaw with.

I thought that maybe Regina was right. But the thought of telling her all about me brought out a cold sweat; the kind of sweat you get when your life is in mortal danger.

Quinten Naylor was at his desk when I called. "What is it, Rawlins?"

"That reward go for me too?"

"If you catch him it does."

"What if he ain't in town?"

"Where is he?"

"Up north."

"Oakland?"

"What makes you ask that? I mean, why wouldn't you think San Francisco?"

"What have you found, Rawlins?" Quinten said in his cop voice.

"I told you 'bout Aretha's and Gregory Jewel an' you couldn't do nuthin' with it, officer. Now I'ma go find the man myself."

Maybe he had something to say about that, but I didn't hear it because I'd hung up the phone.

I called Mouse and told him about the reward. He said to meet him in front of Minnie's at four in the morning.

"Why do you have to go up there?" Regina asked. I was packing a small bag for the two-or-three-day trip.

"I told you. They offerin' fifteen thousand dollars for the ones turn him in. That's a lot of money."

"But you already told them he was up there. Now if they catch him you'll get the money anyway."

What could I say? She was right. But this was a job I'd taken on and I felt that I had to see it through. Anyway, being at home before we got things straight was torture for me. I needed some time away.

"You just wouldn't understand," I said lamely.

"Oh, I understand, all right. You're a crook just like that Mouse. You like criminals and bein' in the street."

"What are you talking about?"

"You think I don't know about you? Is that what you think? Your life ain't no secret, Easy. I heard about you and Junior Fornay and Joppy Shag and Reverend Towne. I can see with my own eyes how you're in business with Mofass and not workin' for him. Baby, you cain't hide in your own house."

"I gotta go an' that's all there is to it," I said. "Anything else we can talk about after I get back."

Regina put her hand on my chest and then brought her fingers together until they were all pointing at me.

We stood still for a moment, her nails poised above my heart.

I wanted to tell her that I loved her but I knew that wasn't what she wanted to hear.

"You got to let a woman see the weak parts, Easy. She gotta see that you need her strength. Woman cain't just be a thing that you th'ow money at. She just cain't be yo' baby's momma."

"I'll let . . ." was all I could say until the pressure of her nails stopped me.

"Shhh," she hissed. "Let me talk now. A woman don't care but that you need her love. You know I got a job an' you ain't ever even asked me fo'a penny. So why do I work? You change the baby and water the lawn and even sew up yo' own clothes. You know you ain't never asked me for a thing, Easy. Not one damn thing."

I always thought that if you did for people they'd like you; maybe even love you. Nobody cared for a man who cried. I cried after my mother died; I cried after my father left. Nobody loved me for that. I knew that a lot of tough-talking men would go home to their wives at night and cry about how hard their lives were. I never understood why a woman would stick it out with a man like that.

TWENTY FOUR

MOUSE WAS SLEEPING in the passenger's seat next to me. The stone and sand cliffs of the California coast loomed on one side with the sun just coming over them. The ocean to our left rose out of its gray sleep into deep blue wonder.

I watched the terns and gulls wheel awkwardly between wisps of morning mist. Cactus pads grew at crazy angles as if they had rooted while tumbling down the mountainside. Bright and tiny purple flowers beamed from succulent vines at the side of the road.

My Chrysler was the only car in sight on the Pacific Coast Highway. I felt exhilarated and strong and ready to put everything in its proper place.

The hum of the engine was in my bones. I could have driven forever.

"Hey, Ease," Mouse croaked.

"You up?"

"Why you grinnin' like that, man?"

"Happy to be alive, Raymond. Just happy to be alive."

He uncurled in his seat and yawned. "You gotta be crazy t'be grinnin' like that tiis time'a mornin'. Damn. It's too early for that shit."

"I got some coffee in a thermos on the backseat. Some toast and jelly sandwiches too."

Mouse attacked the sandwiches and poured a cup of coffee for me. The sun rose over the crest and sparkled on the water's surface. For the first time in a week I was excited without the help of whiskey. But that thought made me want a drink.

We went through Oxnard, Ventura, and Santa Barbara. Highway 1 wended inland and by the coast in turns. It was a snaky pathway taken mostly by cars because Highway 101 was a more direct route between San Francisco and L.A.

We'd been going for some hours before starting to talk. I was happy looking at the scenery, and Mouse's nature was more suited to the nighttime.

When we were two hundred miles up the coast he asked, "What happens up north?"

"J.T. Saunders in Oakland. That's all I know."

"What you wanna do when we find'im?" Mouse asked.

"We don't know nuthin' 'bout him, Raymond. He may be just a bad-luck dude in the wrong place at the wrong time. All we do is watch'im an' give the police his address."

"S'pose he runs?"

"He ain't gonna run."

"What make you say that?"

"He ain't gonna see us so he ain't gonna run."

Mouse nodded and hunched his shoulders. "We'll see," he said.

By twelve we had gone past San Jose and were entering the Santa Cruz mountain range.

"You ever know anybody who went in for the sulfa-drug syphilis cure?" I asked.

"Me."

"What?"

"Me. I went down to that damned place for six months. They had me down for five years."

"And you stopped going?"

"Sure did. Damn! I hated that shit. You know, you go in there an' they give you that shot and the next thing you know you get this foul-assed nasty taste in your mouf. Shit! I hate even thinkin' about it."

"Raymond, you gotta go see a doctor."

"Why?"

" 'Cause syphilis gets all in your body and comes out later on."

"I ain't got syphilis."

"But you just said . . ."

". . . I said that I went in for the treatment. I was a kid and I had this here pimple on my dick. I had this girl, Clovis, who said she wouldn't fuck me so I went to the doctor. He looked at my dick and said, 'Syphilis.' Then they made me go every week for that shot."

"Maybe he could tell just from looking." But I didn't believe that.

"Uh-uh. I know 'cause I got drunk one night and tried t'sign up for the army with Joe Dexter the next mornin'. When it came time to go I went down all smug and told'em that they couldn't take me 'cause I had the syph. But this big ole cracker told me that my tests turned up clear. I ain't never had it."

White doctors at one time thought that almost all Negroes

were rife with veneral disease. I could believe that they wouldn't bother with a test.

"So," I asked. "Why didn't you go into the army?"

"They got my jail record the same day. They said t'come back when the fightin' was worse. It never did get bad enough for them to wanna take me."

The past few years I had been staying at the Galaxy Motel on Lombard. It was only ten dollars a night and the old couple there knew me. Mr. and Mrs. Riley. They were an old Irish couple whose parents had immigrated. They had soft brogues and gentle smiles.

"Well hello, Easy," Mr. Riley greeted me as I came into his glass-walled office. "Haven't seen you in quite a while."

Wine racks on the wall held maps, ferry schedules, and tourist guides to parts of the city.

"Workin' too hard down there. Too hard."

"How's the wife?"

"Fine. How's Mrs. Riley?"

"At home with the grandchildren. Cecily had twins last June."

I checked us into a room with two double beds and a television.

I had Mr. Riley dial Axminister 3-854 from the switchboard. Karl Bender answered. He didn't know a J. T. Saunders and he didn't know me. I tried to find out how long he'd had that phone number and his address but that didn't get me anywhere.

"What now?" Mouse asked.

"I don't know. I got a twenty-year-old address for him."

"Twenty years! Man, I lived in over a hundred places in twenty years."

"And every one of them remembers you."

Mouse's boyish grin was disarming. Not that he needed it; I'd seen him cut down more than one armed man in his day.

It had gotten dark outside. The headlights lined up on the Lombard. Two prostitutes took the room next to ours and started doing business. Mouse and I had to laugh, because they could get a john in and out of that room in five minutes flat. The walls were like paper so we could hear it all.

"Uh-uh, money first," one of the girls would say. You could hear the man breathing and then the rustle of clothes.

"Oh!" she'd cry before he had time to get in her, and then, "Do it!" And the guy would all of a sudden scream or grunt or groan. His tone would always be a little sorry like a rube at a carnival who'd hit the pyramid of milk bottles dead center but couldn't knock them over.

"What you wanna do, Easy?" Mouse said at about eight o'clock. "'Cause you know I gotta do sumpin' or I'ma go give my money to them girls next door."

"Let's go over to Oakland and see where this J. T. Saunders used to live," I said.

"Do it!" one of the girls next door replied.

TWENTY FIVE

WE WENT ACROSS on the lower level of the Bay Bridge. It was Friday night and ten thousand cars followed our example. In the rearview mirror I saw the shimmering lights of San Francisco above the herd of shifting, speeding cars.

Oakland was a full fifteen degrees warmer than San Francisco. We went from comfortable weather to where I had to open the collar of my shirt.

2489 Stockard Street was a three-decker apartment building. The paint had peeled off so long ago that the wood siding had weathered to gray.

A fat woman sat on the porch fanning herself with a church fan. Two small boys ran around her with slats of wood in their hands.

"Bangbangbangbangbangbangbangbang," said one of the boys.

"Kachoom, kachoom," the other one volleyed in deep tones, reminiscent of cannon fire.

The woman was oblivious to the war going on around her. She was very dark with gray hair and a young face.

"Ma'am?" I said. I took two steps up. The boys stopped dead, the slat-guns forgotten in their hands.

The woman kept fanning. She was concentrating on something across the street.

I took another step and said again, "Ma'am?"

The boys' mouths were what my mother used to call flytraps.

"Yes?" She still had her eyes glued out across the street.

I looked in that direction. The only thing I could make out was the shifting light of a TV through a window. I couldn't make out the picture. I doubted that she could either.

"What you want?" the woman asked.

"Does a family named Saunders live around here?"

"No." She leaned forward to show me that she was busy watching.

"Bangbangbang."

"Did a family by that name ever live here?"

"Maybe they did, mister. How you expect me to know?"

The artillery boy was using me for cover. He lobbed charges from his cannon-slat as his nemesis sought cover behind the young-old woman.

I could see Mouse down by the car smoking a cigarette and sitting on the hood.

And I stood there, watching her watch television.

After a minute the woman craned her neck back and cried, "Nate!"

A window opened on a floor above and a raspy voice called out, "Yeah?"

"Man down here wanna know if somebody called . . ." She turned to me and asked, "Whashisname?"

I told her.

"Saunders!" she shouted. "Ever lived here?"

"Come on up," the sandpaper voice said. "Number twenty-seven."

"Sir?" I called from the latched screen of his front door.

Nate, whoever he was, lived in his living room. He had a bed in there and a table with a hot plate and toaster on it. There was a two-tiered bookshelf that was stacked high with pamphlets.

The old man, with the help of two canes, got up slowly from his chair at the window and slowly made it to the door. It was whole minute watching him move the cane in his right hand to his left. I wondered if he had the strength to pop the latch on the door.

"Evenin', young man," he greeted.

We took the long journey back to his chair at the window.

"Hot out, ain't it?" he asked.

I nodded. "How come you got a screen on the front door? You got flies in the building?"

"I like the door open but sometimes them damn kids come in here and steal my cake if I take a nap."

"Oh."

"You interested in the Saunderses, is you?"

"Did you know them?"

"Nathaniel Bly," he said.

I was confused for a moment and then I realized that he was telling me his name.

"Vincent Charles," I replied.

"Why you want them after all these years, Mr. Charles?"

"I knew their son, J.T."

He nodded and my heart jumped a little. "We did some time

in the merchant marines. This is the only address I got for him."

Nate sat there nodding at me. He had a wistful smile on his face almost as if he were remembering something I'd mentioned.

"I don't even know if any'a them is still alive," he said. "His daddy died even before they moved. You know Viola couldn't pay the rent here on such a big apartment. I don't know why somebody want a place so big anyways. I like to have everything right with me. But my chirren pays the rent so I stay here. They live right down here, you know. Willie's on Morton and Betty live on Seventeenth. Willie's a car mechanic in San Francisco an' Betty caterin'. Lotta folks say that caterin' is domestic work and they turn up their nose but Betty could buy and sell mosta them. Last year she made more than ten thousand dollars . . ."

"Did she play with J.T. when they were small?"

The question caught Nate up short. He'd forgotten that I'd come there looking for somebody.

"No," he said. "Willie an' Betty was a couple years younger than J.T. and Squire."

"Squire?"

"I thought you said you was J.T.'s buddy? How come you don't know about his brother?"

I laughed agreeably. "We was on a boat, man. J.T. didn't talk about his family, except this address, and I didn't ask."

"He was somethin' else." Nate shook his head. "Always tor-turin' li'l animals and beatin' up my kids."

"J.T?"

"Squire. J.T. was a timid little boy. He had some kinda fright when he was a baby and he was scared'a all kindsa things—especial-ly bugs. I mean, he couldn't take seein' a ant on the sidewalk. An' Squire'd go out and catch a ole dead dragonfly and run after J.T. with it. And when Viola would come out Squire'd jes' say, 'I try'n give him a pretty.' Sweet and evil, just like a angel from hell.

"One time I come up on them in the basement. Squire was beatin' on J.T. with a piece'a rubber hose. He kept tellin' J.T., 'Do it! Do it!' And finally J.T. whimper and cries and picks up this big half-dead waterbug and puts it down the front of his own pants. You know that poor boy falled down on the ground, cried for all he had. Squire danced around him like a witch. Like a witch."

"Why didn't you stop him, Nate?"

Nate gave me an inquiring look. "Where you from, son?"

"Texas. Texas an' Louisiana."

"Was that hard back then while you was comin' up?" he asked.

I had to grin when I nodded.

"I used to think that Negroes was niggers. And them niggers had to be hard to make it in this here hard world. I always worried that if a child seen me doin' for him he might grow up thinkin' that the world would do for him. I raised my kids hard. And now they pay my rent and drop off the groceries but they ain't never got no time to talk with me. I know they think I was mean."

"But they're doin' all right," I said.

"When I seen Squire torturin' J.T. I told myself that the boy had to learn how to fight. But you know my heart was dancin' along with Squire while that poor boy suffered. It was dancin' up a storm."

He looked out the window after that speech.

After a while I asked, "Do you know where Viola Saunders lives today?"

"Cain't say that I do."

When I got downstairs the boys were eating out of a quart container of ice milk and the woman was still gazing across the street.

None of them looked up to watch me go.

TWENTY SIX

VIOLA SAUNDERS WAS in the phone book: 386¾ Queen Anne's Lane.

Queen Anne's Lane was a short street, only one block in length, that was crowded with apartment buildings. There was a big vacant lot on one side and eight large apartment buildings, built into a hill, on the other.

We went up and down the block but 386¾ wasn't to be found. Finally we went into 386 and knocked on a screen door on the first floor. A television was playing somewhere in the apartment and we could see its shadowy light play down the long dark hallway.

A small boy, almost a baby, came running down the hall. He stopped at the screen and looked up at us.

"Wah!" he exclaimed.

All he wore was a striped T-shirt that barely came down to his distended belly button.

"Arnold!" a woman screamed from inside the house. She came down the hall with a baby in each arm and two more trailing at her skirts.

She was of medium height and attractively built. She wore a muumuu with a neckline cut lower than most, that clung to her figure because of the perspiration. She had slack lips, that accented the carelessness of her eyes, and light skin. Her children were all different colors. The baby we first met was light like his mother but the infants she held were both black, twins. One little girl, who was about five and stood peering at us from behind her mother's right leg, was a solid brown color. Her little sister, on the other side, was almost white with dirty-blond hair and greenish eyes. You could see that they were all siblings by their eyes. They all had their mother's vacant, slightly wondering stare.

The young mother gave me a brief once-over and then she looked at Mouse. He wore a deep blue square-cut shirt that hung out over loose gray trousers. His shoes were gray suede. His smile sparkled from behind the diamond in his front tooth.

"Yeah?" she asked Mouse in a slow, meaningful way.

He smiled, bowed almost imperceptibly, and said, "We lookin' fo'a man named J. T. Saunders. You know 'im?"

"Uh-uh," she said. She didn't care either.

One of the babies started crying and the mother said, "Vanessa, Tiffany, here," and she leaned over to hand the crying baby and his docile brother to the two little girls. "Take Henry an' them back in the big room."

The little girls, both of them almost toppling under the weight of their brothers, staggered back toward the shadowy TV light.

Little Arnold stayed until they were almost around the corner and then he turned to run after.

"You wanna come in?" she asked Mouse. She took the latch

off the screen and we followed her into the hall. We walked down to where the TV was and turned in the opposite direction.

It was a small kitchen lit by a bare sixty-watt bulb. The walls were a greasy yellow. The floor was covered by pitted yellow linoleum. The yellow tile sink was piled high with dishes. There was a big pan of dirty rice, open and crusty, sitting on the two-burner stove. The ceiling, which was once white, was blackened by smoke and grease.

I was the only one who noticed the dirt, though. Our hostess had taken a bottle of beer from her little refrigerator and handed it to Mouse. They weren't talking but their eyes were exchanging promises.

"You know where three eighty-six and three-quarters is?" I asked before they could fall into an embrace.

"Huh?" she asked.

"What's your name?" Mouse asked her.

"Marlene."

"We lookin' fo' three eighty-six and three-quarters, Marlene," Mouse said. He might have been talking about her eyes, or maybe her breasts.

Marlene pointed through a small window above the sink.

"Up there," she said. "It's one'a them."

Through the window I saw a small concrete path that led past 386 to a small bank of houses nestled behind the larger apartment buildings.

Arnold was at the door looking at us. Greenish mucus welled at his left nostril.

Mouse was looking hard at Marlene.

I moved toward the door. I was halfway down the hall when Mouse came after me.

"Wait up, Easy, you cain't go up against him by yo'self," he said.

"I thought you was busy."

Marlene followed us until we were out of the door. Mouse stopped at the door and looked at her meaningfully. "What you doin' later on, Marlene?"

"Nuthin'."

"You mind if I come back?"

"Uh-uh, I be here."

The concrete pathway was dark but there was a half-moon. On the left side of the path an unpainted picket fence protected any strollers from a sixty-foot drop down into the backyard of Marlene's apartment building.

It was a steep climb and Mouse and I were both puffing by the time we made the summit.

There were seven little houses with all kinds of numbers on them.

There was a light on inside 386¾.

Mouse and I looked at each other before going up the short dirt path to the front door. He unbuttoned the two lower buttons of his shirt and shrugged so that he could reach his pistol if he needed it. I went on ahead of him to the door.

A woman answered this door too. She was tall and imposing. She seemed all the more noble because her salt-and-pepper hair was wrapped high on her head with a bright red-and-purple scarf. Her nightdress was a long coral gown. It set off her dark skin in a way that spoke of the islands.

"Yes?" Her voice was musical and deep.

"J.T. here?" I could feel Mouse tense up behind me.

"Who are you?" she asked.

"Martin," I said. "Martin Greer. This is my cousin Sammy." I moved aside to point at Mouse. He smiled.

"Hm! What you want here?"

"We came up from L.A. Abernathy told us we should look up J.T. when we got here."

"Randall Abernathy?"

"Yeah, Randy."

"He don't even like us."

"He didn't say nuthin' like that to me. Matter'a fact he said that J.T. got him a job. Yeah, Randy said that J.T. was good at havin' some fun."

"And what about you?" she asked Mouse. "What do you want?"

"Uh . . . well . . ." Mouse gaped at her. There was a certain kind of woman that just had him cowed. She could have slapped his face and he would have apologized for hurting her hand.

"What do you want?" Viola Saunders asked again. She was older than us, sixty or more, and commanding.

"Could we come inside?" I asked.

For a moment she stared at me. I tried to open my face, to let her know that I was going to be honest with her. Later, when we sat down in her house, I could lie.

Viola opened the door and I felt a touch at my shoulder.

"I'ma wait out here, Ease," Mouse whispered at my ear.

The room she led me to was large but there was very little floor space because of the crowd of furniture. Bookshelves covered with knickknacks and books lined every wall. Two couches, three stuffed chairs, a walnut coffee table, a cherry dining table, and a piano were stabled there. The deep green carpet was thick. It swallowed up the sounds walking might have made. The walls were green too.

"Have a seat, Mr. Greer."

"Thank you, ma'am. You sure have a nice house."

"What do you want with my son?" She stood next to the piano.

"Nuthin' special. I just heard that he knew how to have a good time in Oakland and . . ."

"Don't lie to me, son. What James do to you?"

My muscles went lax and my ability to lie just flowed away from me.

"Nothing to me personally, Mrs. Saunders. But maybe he knows something about a girl he was with a few weeks ago."

"She pregnant?"

"She's dead."

Viola Saunders pulled back on her neck like a viper does before she strikes. Her eyes glassed over and her shoulders rose.

"What her die from?"

"Somebody killed her. She wasn't the only one."

"And you t'ink it were James?"

"All I know is that somebody saw her with him and there was a fight."

The elegant woman from the islands closed her eyes. Her lips went in and out a little and her neck quivered ever so slightly.

"Is James staying here, ma'am?"

"He's a good son, Mr. Greer. He always bring me somet'ing when he goes away. He always bring me somet'ing."

The house was empty, silent and sad.

"He's a good son," she said again. "But he's different now. It's like he's not himself no more. He get so angry sometimes that I worry. I lock my door against him, sometimes. My own son."

I knew that she'd tell me anything I wanted as long as I let her talk.

"You going to hurt my son, Mr. Greer?" She used my fake name to have power over me. Even that one lie was almost too much to bear.

"No, ma'am."

"What about your friend?"

"We just want to talk to him, that's all."

"He was always a gentle boy."

"Do you know where I could find him?"

"I don't want to hear that you hurt my boy 'cause I help you, Mr. Greer."

"I just want to ask him what happened."

"Was it a young girl?"

"Yeah, she was seen with your son but nobody says that he killed her. I just want to ask him a few questions."

Mrs. Saunders trusted me. But she was worried.

"If I tell him about this he will be warned, Mrs. Saunders. He'll know that he was the last one to see her."

"You find him at Tiny Bland's. It's down there on Chino Street near Lake Merritt. He go down there for the whores on Friday."

Viola walked with me out into the front yard.

"You let my son be, hoodlum," she said to Mouse.

He scuffed his toe on the sidewalk and watched the ground. "Yes, ma'am."

"Look at me," Viola demanded.

Mouse looked her in the eye; the fact of him feeling fear frightened me.

"Don't you hurt my son."

"You got it." Mouse nodded and turned away.

When she had gone back into the house Mouse relaxed again. He was fully calm as we descended toward the street.

"You think Marlene wanna go with us?" he asked when we'd gotten to the car.

"I think she got five kids need a momma stay with'em, Raymond."

He scratched his chin and said, "Yeah. You right." Then he smiled. "I come back after they in bed."

TWENTY SEVEN

THE BROAD RED neon sign said Tiny Bland's in bold script. It shone behind a black glass wall that made up the facade of the nightclub.

Cars drove up letting out fancy Negro men and Negro women dressed in furs and silk. The women also wore gaudy costume jewelry and carried bags made of soft leather.

Across the street winos shambled and skinny teenagers played. Two young men in T-shirts and jeans leaned against an old Chevrolet and eyed the patrons of Tiny Bland's with sullen stares. The kind of stares that say, "I wanna fuck you or kill you or eat you." Or maybe all three.

But the club-goers weren't bothered. They were telling jokes and laughing. Two weeks' pay went into one evening at Tiny Bland's.

A tall black man wearing a metallic gold suit stood at the front door. He greeted the patrons and warded off any undesirable element that might seek entry.

A young man who worked parking the cars was at the bouncer's beck and call. He wore a dark blue uniform with gold satin stripes along the sides of his pants. He was full of "yessir" and "yes'm." He had more teeth than all of those smiling women. He had a pocketful of tip change and his body danced with expectations.

"How we gonna get in here?" I asked Mouse. "I didn't think our boy'd go someplace like this."

Mouse shrugged. "Just walk in the front door, man, like everybody else."

"We ain't dressed fo'it, Raymond."

But Mouse ignored me. He got on the short line that had formed at the door. I stood there with him, glad that we were going to be refused entry. I had sobered a little and thought that we'd do better following Saunders at a distance. We could wait across the street with the winos and muggers and follow our quarry to wherever he lived.

The doorman was letting a couple up at the front of the line go in. It was an orangish Negro, who sported a crew cut, and his blond date. Everybody on the line was let in.

Until the guard laid eyes on me, that is.

I was wearing ocher slacks and a gray shirt that had two tiny cigarette holes in the pocket.

He looked at those holes like they might have been plague warts and asked, "Yeah? What you want?"

"I wanna come in. You got air conditioning in there?"

"Don't matter if I do, 'cause you ain't comin' in." He looked over my shoulder, indicating that our audience was through and that he was ready for the next applicant.

"Open that do', man, fo' I put you' head th'ough it." That was Mouse.

He hadn't noticed Mouse before. Maybe he thought that the short one was my ugly date.

Anyway, he looked down then and said, "What?"

"You heard me, Leonard, I said open up that door."

Mouse had a big grin on his face. The man in the gold suit was grinning too.

"Mouse," he said.

"Thatta be Mr. Mouse to you." They shook hands and laughed some.

Then Mouse asked, "Man, what they got you wearin'?"

Leonard spread a big hand across his golden chest and looked down shyly.

"That's what they pay me for, brother," he said.

"I hear ya," Mouse intoned.

We were waved in.

The hostess at the podium was black. As were the waiters, the musicians on the platform up front, and most of the patrons.

Mouse asked for a table but I interrupted and said that we'd stand at the bar for a while.

I ordered a triple shot of scotch. Mouse ordered beer.

"Nice place, huh, Easy?"

He was grinning and looking around the room. It was a large room with low ceilings, painted black from the floor up. The waitresses wore white satin gowns and the waiters wore tuxedos.

There were people and more people. The band was playing upbeat jazz, not like the religious refrains of Lips McGee. A crystal globe hung in the center of the room throwing off bright fragments of light that made everything seem a little unreal. Maybe Tiny Bland's was worth two weeks' pay.

"How'd you know that dude?" I asked Mouse.

"I hung out here for a while."

"When?"

"When Terry Peters got kilt."

It was in the street that Mouse had killed Terry in a dispute over two thousand dollars.

"How long you up here?"

"Until somebody else got killed and the cops started worryin' 'bout that."

The bar was long and shiny black. A few feet down from us, Crew Cut was drinking and telling a story to his white date.

She was making eyes at the man next to them.

I don't know if the woman wanted to start trouble but she was well on her way with that flirtation. The man she was making eyes at was of normal height but you could tell by looking at him that he was brawny and full of violence. He had shaggy hair and a thin mustache. His eyes were murky and unfocused even though he stared directly in the white woman's face. But none of these features matched the gash in his neck. There was a wide and jagged scar at his throat, made all the more unsightly because it was lighter, yellowish actually, than his medium-brown skin.

I wondered what kind of accident or war could have caused such a catastrophe. I was more than a little awed that this burly fellow, or anyone, could have survived that pain and bloodletting.

But he just smiled and flirted with the white woman while Crew Cut talked about how he had installed a shortwave radio in his Pontiac.

"Easy," Mouse said. I turned back to him. He was looking around the room.

"Yeah?"

"He ain't here, man."

"We ain't even looked good yet, Raymond."

"I looked."

"You mean you wanna get back to that sloppy girl's house. That's what you mean."

Mouse beamed and smoothed his mustache. "I know what's waitin' back at home, man."

"An' what if she got a boyfriend come in at twelve? What you gonna do then?"

"I do what I do, Easy. An' you know I do it good."

"Hey, man, back off," someone behind me declared. It was said with such anger that I turned quickly and took a step back.

The orange man was pulling his date's hand from the scarred man's caress. The scarred man held his hands out, palms up, and smiled just like Mouse had smiled. I felt the force of the triple shot hit my hands; they felt weak and impotent.

The woman in front of me got out of the way but I was too slow. The scarred man flipped his right hand over and made it into a fist that went crashing into Crew Cut's face. The next thing I knew I was being struck in the chest by the orange man's back. His fuzzy head was at my chin. He pushed against me and went back up against his foe.

It was a mistake he paid for.

By the time he was on the floor he was bleeding from the mouth and nose. There was a circle around the two men. Nobody moved for a brief moment. The orange man was panting on his back, propped up by both elbows. The scarred man was in a crouch with a vacant look in his face. The last time I had seen a look like that was in the Battle of the Bulge. It was on a German foot soldier who intended to send me to hell.

The scarred man reached into his gray jacket.

The orange man smiled.

The scarred man came out with short thick-bladed knife and took a step.

Somebody screamed.

The orange man took out a pistol and pointed it.

I could see the knife-wielder's eyes change. He was defeated and the murder was gone from him; maybe he even started to lower the blade.

I'll never know, because the smiling orange man began pulling off shots. At the first shot the scarred man started to genuflect. Pow! . . . and a cursory bow. Pow! . . . and chin comes down to hide the scar. By the sixth shot he was prostrate over his knees on the floor.

The orange man never stopped smiling.

People were either running or kissing the floor. One very fat woman in a vast sky-blue gown tried to squeeze herself down into a corner. I saw the orange man's date run out the front door, but her boyfriend hardly moved.

After a few moments he got to his feet. He dusted himself off in a ritual fashion, slightly patting his forearms and knees. He put the gun in his pocket and sat down at the bar. The room had almost emptied out by then.

"Com'on, man, let's get outta here," Mouse said at my side. "Cops be here any minute. An' you know I ain't gonna answer no questions when I could be with Marlene."

Being at the scene of a murder meant no more to Mouse than a dead cow meant to Randall Abernathy. All us poor southern Negroes had lived and breathed death since we were children, but Mouse was different—he accepted it. To him death was as natural as rain.

I agreed that we should leave but I was bothered by the murder. Everything seemed logical. I mean, one man has been killing the other over women for a hundred thousand years. But why didn't he even look for his date? Why didn't he run?

Outside we joined the crowd across the street. I thought that we might catch a glimpse of Saunders.

The ambulance was there in under ten minutes. The police

were there before that. They hustled the killer off. I couldn't be sure but the orange man's hands seemed to be free. Unshackled.

While Mouse talked to the doorman I moved around looking for the bearded man. I didn't catch sight of him.

I did see the two toughs who were eyeing the club earlier. They were talking to some of the men from the club. Thinking that they might know why the killing was so unusual I moved near to them and listened.

At first a big man in a tan cotton suit was talking.

He said, "Yeah. The short-haired dude seen that man you said holding on to his girl's hand. You know he was lookin' right down her dress an' lickin' his lips . . ."

"Yeah, yeah," a smaller, mutt-faced man said. "I'da kilt him too. You see that? Guy says leggo my-my girl and here-here he go kickin' his ass. Th-that ain't right."

"Yow main," said one of the T-shirts. "Sand'r'n them allus like'n take it. Shit, he fock my cousin an' a'most kilt Bobby Lee."

"Who you said that was?" I asked the boy.

He glared at me because of my tone. Maybe I reminded him of his truant officer.

"Sander," he said, almost swallowing the word.

"Did he useta wear a beard?" I held my hand under my chin to show him what I meant.

"Yeah."

"Where he from?"

"Who the fuck're you, man?" the other boy shouted.

The mutt-faced man and his friend walked away. I remember thinking that they were smart men. I thought that I'd never do this kind of work again.

Then I thought about fighting those youngsters. They were in their late teens, maybe one was older. The one on the left had well-defined arms in the lamplight. I was still young enough that

I could take them. I might have gotten a bloody nose but those boys' lives were in my hands.

They moved apart, watching my hands and eyes. Maybe they did this for a living. More probably for fun.

I reached into my pocket and pulled out two five-dollar bills, handing one to each of them.

"Where'd you say that man Saunders was from? I mean where was he born?" I asked.

"He talk funny," the first boy said. He snatched the bill at the same as his partner did.

"Yeah," the other boy said. "He always say 'mon' insteada 'main.'"

"He been gone for a while?" I asked them. But now that they had my five dollars they had somewhere to go. I could see it in their eyes again.

"Hell, main, I ain't been' paid t'watch that crazy mothah-fuckah. Shit!"

With that they both took off.

TWENTY EIGHT

I WAS THINKING about what I had to say while the phone rang. The girls next door were having a party with two men and the neon light from the motel sign was flashing through the gauzelike curtains.

Mouse was at Marlene's house. I'd let him off there.

"Hello?" Quinten's voice was thick.

"Sorry t'be botherin' you, man, but I got somethin'."

"Where you calling from?"

"San Francisco."

"You find Saunders?"

"Yeah, I found'im."

"It's late, Easy. I don't have time to play with you."

His father probably said the same words when Quinten was just a baby cop.

"He's dead."

"Where?"

"Probably in the morgue over in Oakland."

"You sure?"

"Pretty much so. I saw'im get shot. I saw them carry him off with a sheet over his eyes."

"Who killed him?"

"Nobody I know. The police got him too."

There was a silence on the other end of the line. Maybe I was needlessly worrying about how the man I sought out in another city was murdered before my eyes.

"You go to police headquarters office downtown, in Oakland, at about noon. Where are you now?"

I gave him the number of the motel.

"You be at police headquarters at noon unless I call you to say something else."

"Okay, Quinten. All right, man. I'll be there. But if this is the dude I want the reward and I want you people to get off my ass and to stay off it too."

"Noon," he said and then he hung up.

"Hello." Her voice was soft and sweet and inviting.

"Hey, honey, I wake you?"

"Easy?"

"Yeah, baby."

"When you comin' home?"

"Prob'ly not till day after tomorrow. Around dinner. Did I get you outta bed?"

"No."

"You up at midnight?"

"I couldn't sleep so I was cleanin' the kitchen."

"I love you, honey. You know I got a lot t'tell when I get home."

"Okay," she said so softly that I almost didn't hear.

"You know I got money, baby, but it's yours too. I never . . ."

"Tell me when you get here, Easy."

"Cain't we talk now?"

"I don't wanna talk like this, on the phone. You come on home, Easy."

"I love you," I said.

"We'll talk when you get home," she whispered back.

The next morning found me at Marlene's apartment door.

"Momma an' them in the bedroom," the dirty-blond girl told me. She had the disdain of a woman in her voice. She was learning early to hate men for their indifference, and to lament the treachery of her mother.

"Will you tell the man, Mouse, something for me?"

She just stared at the floor.

I took a silver fifty-cent piece from my pocket and handed it to her.

Her frown never left her face but her eyes widened and she took the coin. She started to run but I touched her arm.

"You tell him that I will be back at four. Okay?"

" 'kay," she told my wrist. Then she ran hard into the house calling her sister's name.

"Ezekiel Rawlins," I told Miss Cranshaw for the third time.

"How do you spell that?" the gray-haired, stick-figured old secretary asked.

"I don't know."

"What?"

"I ain't never been to school an' my momma us'ly signs all my papers. Ain't nobody evah axed me t'spell it at all really. You the first one."

I had been standing there in my best brown suit with a cream-colored shirt, real gold cufflinks, brown blucher shoes, and argyle socks. I had on a hand-painted silk tie, double-knotted to perfection. And this woman had called everybody but me. I had been there, and in the chair in front of her, for over an hour.

I had told her, in my best white man's English, "I would like to be announced to the chief's office. I know that this is an unusual request, but a police officer from Los Angeles, a Sergeant Quinten Naylor, told me to meet him, with the chief, concerning a case in Los Angeles that seems to overlap with a case in your lovely city."

"You should go to your own precinct to give information you have there, sir," she said and then opened a drawer to look in, giving me a chance to withdraw.

I insisted.

She asked me my name.

I gave it, and spelled it, and she called the aide to the captain of precinct we were in.

She told me that he had never heard of me.

I restated my speech.

She asked me my name.

We might have gotten to hate each other if one of the aides to the assistant mayor hadn't been informed that there actually was an L.A. cop in with the chief. They were waiting on an informant from L.A.

Miss Cranshaw almost spit bile as she made the call for me. Her jaws clenched so that I thought her teeth might crack.

It might have been the first time she'd had to serve a Negro. I was working for progress.

"Is this the man you were looking for from Los Angeles?" Chief Wayland T. Hargrove asked me.

We were in the Oakland City morgue standing over a lab table that bore the remains of J.T. Saunders. He was naked and mottled. He smelled sour like old vegetables smell just before they sprout fungus.

His eyes were open and his head turned slightly toward the left. The gash in his neck was less pronounced in death.

"I think he is, sir," I said. "He certainly is the one I saw getting shot. I saw the man that shot him too. I don't know whether I'd call it self-defense or what."

"No need to bother about that," spectator Bergman from the governor's office said. He appeared at the Oakland morgue a few minutes after we did. "What we want to know is if this is the man who killed those women in the South Bay."

"You mean in L.A."

"No, Easy," Quinten Naylor said. "There were three murders up here last year. This man is a suspect."

"Black women?"

"All of them." Quinten was looking me straight in the eye. He wanted me to keep quiet, and I knew why. He had to answer for the murders in L.A. before hysteria eroded his ability to work there. Trouble with Wayland T. Hargrove or, more especially, Mr. Bergman was the last thing he needed.

But I was mad. "What?"

Chief Hargrove lifted his eyebrows at my indignation. He was wearing gray pinstripes and had a headful of blue-gray hair.

"This man has been a problem in the Bay for fifteen years," Hargrove said to no one in particular. "He spent five years away for manslaughter. He was suspected in the killing of his first wife but there was no evidence. We'd even brought him in on these mutilation killings, but . . ."

"You mean women been gettin' killed up here the same way and nobody knows?"

"That's why the governor had me go to Los Angeles, Mr. Rawlins," Mr. Bergman said. "We were aware of the killings in Oakland, but when it started down in Los Angeles too we became nervous."

" 'Specially when he started in on white girls," I sneered.

"It was prudent, Mr. Rawlins, to keep the investigation secret. We had no hard evidence that it was a single perpetrator."

I was quiet because it took every ounce of willpower I had to keep from tearing that head from those shoulders.

"We understand," Roland Hobbes said. "All we want is to lift this guy's prints and check them against the ones we got at the site of the Scott killing."

"Of course," the chief said. "Of course."

"What about the guy killed this man?" I asked.

"That's Oakland police business," said Bergman.

"I saw it, man. I saw it, and it looked like a setup to me."

"Watch it, Easy," Naylor said under his breath. "You're just a guest here."

"Ain't you guys here to find crime and stop it? What if that other guy was part of it?"

"He wasn't," the spectator said.

"How do you know?"

"He's a cop."

He might as well have hit me with a sledgehammer. My brain turned to jelly. My heart almost stopped in my chest.

Bergman's any-color eyes complemented the smile he aimed at me.

"A cop?"

The chief cleared his throat. "I hope you men get what you need here," he said. "If there's anything else I can do for you, please ask. Give my regards to Mr. Voss and Captain Violette."

He turned, as did his entourage of two plainclothes bodyguards, two uniformed policemen, and the assistant. Bergman, the porcelain devil, accompanied them. Quinten Naylor, Roland Hobbes, and I were left with a white-coated morgue assistant and a diminutive doctor who'd come in from a game of golf to oversee this postmortem.

"Do you have the materials you need?" the little doctor asked Quinten.

"Um," Quinten answered, looking rather squeamishly at the corpse.

"I'll do it," Roland Hobbes said.

He began bringing out fingerprinting paraphernalia from a small tan suitcase that he carried. Quinten touched my arm and said, "Let's talk outside for a minute."

In the morgue corridor Quinten looked a little healthier. He wasn't so afraid of dead people as long as he didn't have to touch them.

"It's over, Easy," he said in the wide green hall.

"It is?"

"For you. There might be questions. There might be an investigation as to the killing of Saunders. But you've done your job. You can stay here if you want, but I don't think you'll be welcome. I don't think you'll be welcome at all."

I thought of Marlene opening the door for Mouse. She welcomed him.

"What about the reward?"

"It's got to be verified, but if the investigation points at this guy then the money is yours."

"Me and Mouse. He's been lookin' with me."

Quinten frowned. "Where is he?"

"Where he belongs. More than I can say for us."

"Well." Quentin wouldn't meet my gaze. "We're gone after this. You want tickets to fly home?"

"I got a car, and some unwelcome questions to ask."

"They'll kill you up here, Easy. It's just that simple."

"Who sent that man, Quinten?"

"I don't know. I called Violette and he called Voss and Bergman. After that there was a meeting down at city hall and a call was made to Oakland. Nobody asked me a thing."

TWENTY NINE

QUEEN ANNE'S LANE was ugly in the light of day. People sat out in front of their apartments staring at me. They would have stared at each other if I wasn't there. Children screamed and ran in the empty lots across the street. Boys played war while the little girls watched, half in envy and half bewildered.

I went up to Marlene's apartment building. I was about to go in when I remembered why we had come there in the first place. So instead of going back to the apartment of dirty children. I went up the slender cement passageway to the address we'd looked up the day before.

The door was open and an old woman sat in front of it in a lawn chair. Behind her I could see people, mainly women moving quietly about the house.

"Yah?" the old woman said.

"Hi." I smiled and folded my hands in front of me. "I came to see Mrs. Saunders."

"An' why is that?"

I remembered the stick-figured Miss Cranshaw. She was white and this woman black, but they both had the same regard for me.

"I was here last night and she sent me down to deliver a message to James. I didn't get to talk with him but I saw him get killed."

Gray hairs battled with nappy white ones across the woman's head. There was a bald patch toward the top of her pate.

"What's your name?"

For a moment I froze, forgetting completely the name I had used. But then it came to me and I smiled. "Greer. Martin Greer."

"Don't you know your own name?" the elder lady asked. And I wondered if her mother had entertained a man like Mouse while she cared for her little brother.

I wondered but I didn't answer. Finally the woman got up and went back into the house. She took her chair with her and closed the front door.

When the door opened again I was ashamed. The woman from the night before wore an expansive black dress that came down to her bare feet. She was widest at the thighs and her eyes were swollen and vulnerable.

I was a dog.

"Yes?" she said, holding her chin up.

"I was here last night."

"I remember, Mr. Greer. But he's dead now. I can't send you to him now." If she'd cried I would have had to run. I couldn't comfort this woman.

"I know," I said. "I saw it. I saw it all."

"Why didn't you do something?" The tears stayed in her eyes.

"It was too fast . . ."

She nodded.

"It was like, like . . . I don't know . . ."

She put her hand out and I moved out of range.

"Tell me what happened," she said softly.

I did tell her. And as I talked I wondered again if I really was the cause of this fine woman's anguish.

"But you say that he had the gun and he was holding it on James Thomas?"

"Yeah."

"But why would he shoot him?"

"I don't know."

"No. No," she echoed.

"I went down to the police department to make a statement today. They said that they had been looking for J.T. havin' to do with some dead women in the South Bay."

She just looked at me.

"They said that he's the one who killed those girls down in L.A." I said.

I told her the dates of the last killings.

"It couldn't have been."

"He was here?"

"Not all those times, but the last one you said. He was here with me that day. All day."

"You sure?"

"He was right here with me."

Marlene kissed Mouse goodbye with such passion that I felt it across the room. Mouse had a way of bringing out the love in people. It was because there was no shame in him. For the desperate souls in us all, Mouse was the savior. He brought out the dreams you had as a baby. He made you believe in magic again.

He was the kind of devil you'd sell your soul to and never regret the deal.

We went back to the hotel and had fried chicken and broiled ribs from a stand called Fat Charlie's. It was Sunday night, so Ed Sullivan was on television.

The food tasted like cardboard and the stories and acts didn't make any sense.

"What's wrong with you, Easy?" Mouse asked after we ate.

The women were working next door, but slower, as it was the Sabbath. There was a mild groan from the wall and an unconvincing "Ooo, baby."

"Ain't nuthin' wrong."

"No? Then why you droopin' like a puppy just got weaned?"

"They kilt'im, man."

"Kilt who?"

"Saunders. They used me t'set'im up."

"Who did?"

"I really don't know. Maybe it was Quinten or one'a them men he took t'my house. Maybe it was all of'em. Probably was. Somebody killed'im, though. They got his name from me an' killed him."

"So?" Mouse was already bored with talking about my problems.

"So that makes it my fault. That's so."

"He killed them girls, right?" Mouse sighed. "I mighta killed'im my own self if I'da thought about it."

"But he shoulda gone to court. People up here shoulda found out that some man was killing' women and nobody even knew about it. That's probably why they killed him. They didn't want a trial to let people know that a killer had run free and nobody even knew."

"He's dead, Easy. It's over, man."

"But it ain't right."

"Naw, it ain't that. It ain't never right, Ease. Niggah ain't gonna get nuthin' right till they put'im under six feet of loose dirt. That's as right as it gets round these parts."

"So you sayin' I should just drop it?"

"What else can you do?"

"I didn't drop it when you was in jail, Raymond. I got you outta there."

"Uh-huh. An' I thank you fo'that too. But you know we partners, brother. Shit! You better not fuck wit' my partner or I put you down."

There was nothing to argue about. Mouse didn't understand guilt or abstract responsibility. He'd go up against a platoon of men to protect me or EttaMae, his ex-wife, or their boy La-Marque. He'd shoot it out with the law for his own people, but Mouse couldn't hold a moral concept in his brain. Explaining right to him was like trying to explain the color red to a man who was born blind.

And he was right anyway. I tried my best. I did what I thought was right. I found the man killing black women. I did it all.

I couldn't take on the cops. I'd never work for them again, but that's all I could do. I had a wife and children of my own to look after. And Saunders was a killer; I knew that from the moment I laid eyes on him.

We went to sleep early, but Mouse got up in the middle of the night. He sat at the foot of his single bed and smoked a cigarette. I listened to him breathe and to the women talking to each other through the wall.

After a while Mouse went out the door. A moment later I heard a woman's voice say, "Who's there?"

"It's your neighbor," Mouse said. "I brought a bottle'a Jim Beam."

The door opened and the ladies laughed. They partied until six in the morning. Toward the end the women wanted to go to sleep. Finally they sent Mouse back home to me.

THIRTY

THE RIDE DOWN the Coast Highway was beautiful. Mouse slept almost the whole time.

Between the motor humming and the sea air coming in my window I started feeling better about J. T. Saunders. He was a killer, after all, and I had my life to go back to. It was wrong for the police to cover up the killings but I couldn't change the world.

It was a windy afternoon. White rags tore from the navy-blue sea. There was a sonic boom somewhere around Ventura. That roused Mouse for a moment.

"What was that?" he asked.

"Nuthin'. You must' been havin' a dream."

He gave a big grin and said, "Know what I'ma do, Easy?"

"What?"

"First thing I get that money I'ma buy me a '57 T-Bird."

I didn't argue with him. Mouse knew how to enjoy his life.

I got home at about five. Regina's car wasn't parked out front yet. Gabby Lee and Edna weren't to be seen. Jesus' scooter lay on its side near the garden. Everything looked very good.

I had owned that house for more than ten years, but since Regina had moved in, it was more like a home than ever.

I still remember the day I met her. It was at a club in Compton. I was following a man named Addison Prine for his fiancée's father. The old man, Tony Spigs, was sure that Addison had a girlfriend and he wanted me to find her name. Spigs was a jealous old man and he wanted to keep his only daughter at home as long as he could. Spigs was also Mofass' preferred carpenter and I thought I could get a good carpentry job out of him for a hefty favor.

Addison was at a small table with another man and a woman. Near to them a woman sat alone. She was wearing a simple brown dress. She had the dregs of a bright red drink with a straw in it before her.

"Can I sit here?" I asked her in a businesslike manner.

She looked up at me and her eyes laughed. That's when I fell in love. Her eyes laughed without a smile crossing her lips. Then she looked around the room. There were quite a few empty tables around, because it was late afternoon and the Toucan was still waiting for its crowd.

"I like this one," was my answer to her gaze.

She looked the other way and I sat down.

Addison put his hand over the hand of the woman at his table. A waiter came up and took my whiskey order.

Regina didn't avoid my face but she just looked straight ahead, past me rather than at me.

"No, Nancy," Addison said. "I ain't gonna forget you. I got the tickets right-chere in my pocket."

The woman, a chesty specimen in a checkered dress suit, laughed. I thought about Addison's fiancée. Iona Spigs was a pretty but tight-mouthed girl. She liked a neat house and church-filled Sundays.

Nancy liked to get her hands dirty. When she leaned over to kiss Addison it was with her smile showing.

I shook my head and sighed.

My fake date glanced at me, but no more.

I sipped my drink.

Nancy swabbed Addison's mouth with her tongue.

I motioned for the waiter to come over. When he stood there before me I asked my wife-to-be, "Would you like something else?"

She nodded at her empty glass and the waiter went away.

I sighed again.

"What would you do?" I asked my glass.

"What?"

"What would you do if you had a friend and his daughter was gonna marry that man over there?" I swung my head in Addison's direction.

The eyes did their laugh.

"Is that your friend's daughter he kissin'?"

"Not hardly."

She laughed for real then. It was a good laugh in a woman. She let her head fall backward and her mouth open wide. Then she bent forward and thrummed the table with her short, un-painted nails.

I laughed too. Not quite as hard. The waiter brought our drinks.

"I don't think you should do nuthin'," Regina said.

"Why not?" I asked.

"She picked that man. She got a reason that maybe even she don't know."

"But what if he break her heart?"

"She live with her daddy?"

"Yeah."

"At least she be on her own then. Maybe that's what she wants."

Jesus was sitting at the kitchen table. His hands were out in front of him and there was no food or anything else there. He looked up at me when I tousled his hair.

"Run on outside now. Go on an' play, boy. You shouldn't be inside," I said.

I was glad that Regina and Edna were still gone. I had them with me anyway. I enjoyed the feeling of them in the house. On the couch that Edna always jumped from. At the sink where Regina cleaned every night.

"I'm a poor woman and from a long line of proud poor people," she told me that night. I'd told Tony Spigs that I couldn't find anything on Addison.

Regina wasn't an inventive lover. She didn't do tricks or bellow or jibber. But when we came together it was like everything she had was mine. She came on me like waves on the shore. She was constant and strong.

There was a folded piece of paper on the TV. Under the note lay the nine hundred dollars I'd given her. When I saw the money I knew I was lost.

Dear Easy:

It is hard for me to say honey but I found a man that I love. And I am going away with him. You know I have tried but I cannot stay.

You are wonderful Easy but I need something that we don't have. I love you. I do love you but I have to go.

Don't hate me for taking Edna. She needs her mother.

Goodbye.

The dictionary was on the coffee table. She'd looked up the words she couldn't spell. The tears came and my knees buckled. After a long while I looked up and saw Jesus sitting on his haunches. He was sitting watch over me.

THIRTY ONE

I WENT TO the Safeway market the next morning and bought a gallon of vodka and an equal amount of grapefruit soda. Jesus slipped off to school and I drank. I drank deliberately as if I were working.

Lift hand to lip and sip, swallow and sip again, put glass on table but don't let it go. After twenty-one double-sips, refill and start over.

I slept in the afternoon.

Jesus came back at about three-thirty. He came banging in the front door and ran across to his room dropping books and clothes as he went. When he came back I grabbed him by the arm and hefted him into the air.

"What the hell do you think this is, boy, a pigsty?"

He shied away from me after that. I felt wrong about handling him that way but whenever it bothered me I just drank some more.

The phone rang at four. Jesus ran in from the front. He stared worriedly after the bell. I kept up the sipping regimen. Double-sip, ring, double-sip, ring. Finally the phone stopped ringing but the liquor still flowed.

Jesus had warmed two cans of spaghetti for our dinner. I sat at the table but the smell made my stomach lurch. I leaned away from the smell in my chair.

There was a song playing in my head, "I Cover the Water-front." I was humming the lyrics when I looked up and saw Mouse. He appeared as if by magic right there in my dinette.

"Hey, Easy," Mouse said.

Jesus jumped out of his chair and hugged the crazy killer-man.

"Mouse," I replied. I wasn't actually seeing double but Mouse's visage shimmied a little. My voice, and his, carried the slight quality of an echo chamber.

"Better sit up, man. That's how Blackfoot Whitey died."

"What?"

"Sittin' back, drunk in his chair, till he went too far one day an' busted his neck."

"She's gone, man."

"Yeah. I know."

"You do? How'd you find out?"

There were very few times that Mouse actually looked seri-ous. The only times I had ever seen him somber was when he was getting ready to go out on a criminal job. So his grave stare made me wonder, almost forget my sorrow.

"It was Dupree," he said.

I watched my eyelids flutter. My heart did the same. I tried to think of her in that big man's arms. I tried to think of her not with me.

"He been after her at the hospital. You know how he always be bad-mouthin' California . . ."

"How you know?"

"Sophie said it. She was mad that a brother of hers could do that to a friend. She told me so I could tell you."

Up until that moment Regina was still with me. I still loved her and wanted her back. I planned to follow her first letter and beg for her to come back to me. But the thought of her in Dupree Bouchard's arms tainted my brain. There was a smell and an ugly color that became a part of everything we had been. I was sick.

Jesus was at my side with his slender boy's arm around my neck. He put his face against my cheek.

"Mind if I mix me one, Easy?" Mouse asked. He was already pouring a drink.

I nodded and bowed. My wife had left me, had taken my child, had gone off with my friend. There was no song on the radio too stupid for my heart.

That night is still mixed up in my mind. I remember Mouse getting me outside to see his canary-yellow '57 T-Bird. It was a classic from the day it came off the line.

He told me that a loan shark fronted him the money; that he couldn't wait for the reward to buy his new car.

I remember women's breasts held barely in check by loose blouses, and how seeing that sight made me sick inside.

I remember loud music and dancing so hard that my clothes were soaked through with sweat.

I remember a man with tears in his eyes and a kitchen knife in his hand. He was coming toward me. I moved to put my arm out but then I saw that I had my arm around a woman. She yelled in my ear, "Derek! Stop!"

There were other images but most of them were even less coherent. I saw Mouse smiling next to me in the car. He was driving fast and the night wind tore across my face. I was laughing too.

"Ohhhhh, Daddy," came a woman's voice. "Uh, uh, uh."

Every utterance pounded pain right in the center of my brain. I opened my eyes and saw that a woman was lying against my chest. Her dark face was barely visible under the straightened metallic-gold hair. But I could see that she was sleeping.

"Oh yeah yeah," the voice came again. The bed shook and bobbed.

I looked to my left and saw a woman I had never seen before. Her face could have been ugly or beautiful but I couldn't tell because it was contorted in the throes of a powerful orgasm. She was on her side with her eyes looking directly into mine but I don't think I registered for her. Above her left shoulder Mouse was grinning like a hound. His gaze was locked to her profile and his whole body hunched rhythmically while she moaned.

I sat up, pushing the woman on my chest aside. I climbed to the foot of the bed and walked across the sloppy room toward the door.

"Oh, yeah," Mouse called.

The woman yelled out something too but it didn't make any sense, like maybe it was a foreign language.

Outside the door I saw, in the very early morning light, a bathroom.

Even urinating made me feel sick. I could feel the puckered walls of my stomach with every motion. Even breathing made me salivate.

There was a box next to the bathroom door. I kicked it slightly upon leaving the toilet. Any contact sent pains rolling through my head. I put my hand to my eyes and the baby started crying. The baby that had been sleeping in the cardboard box on the floor.

I lifted the child, who was even younger than my own. I kicked open the door to the bedroom and shouted, "Who left this here baby on the flo'?"

Mouse and his girl were still cupped together, but peacefully. When the other woman heard the baby crying she sprang up to her hands and knees and stared at me.

She said, "Who?"

"This baby yours?" I asked, none too kindly.

She ran at me and took the baby away. "Mothah-fuckah!" There was a slight slur to her voice but the hatred was pure.

"Why you gonna leave a baby on the floor, in the toilet?" I yelled.

She swung from side to side looking for a place to deposit her child.

"Bastid!" she yelled. "I kill you!"

We were both naked and not very far from being drunk.

"They should take that baby away from you," I screamed.

The look on the young mother's face was indecipherable. Her lips and eyes squirmed and shook, her whole body vibrated, and the baby hollered.

Mouse came right at me. He had our clothes in his arms. He rammed his body into mine and I fell out of the room. He slammed the door on the two women and threw me my clothes.

"Put 'em on, Easy."

I could still hear the baby crying through the door. I would have never put my child in harm's way.

In the car Mouse drove a few blocks without saying anything. I couldn't have spoken if I wanted to.

But at Crenshaw he stopped the car at the curb. It was no later than five-thirty and the traffic was still light.

"Easy, I gotta talk to you, man."

I sighed.

"You cain't keep up like this, man. All this drinkin' an' feelin' sorry fo' yo'self. I mean, it's done, man. The man is dead and the woman is gone."

I thought about Bonita Edwards sitting so peacefully by the tree. Mouse pulled out into the street and drove me home.

I never said a word and he didn't say anything else.

I stood out in front of the house for a while before going in.

Jesus was sleeping on the couch. He had some of Edna's toys around him on the floor. He used one of her baby pillows for his own head.

THIRTY TWO

LAID IN bed with my eyes open wide. At least that's how it felt. I must have been dreaming, though, because people were coming in and out of my room, bad-mouthing me. Regina came, and Saunders and Quinten Naylor. Everybody had something to say and I was in no condition to contradict them.

I watched the windowpane go from day to night.

There was a large, jagged stone in my lower intestines and my fingers were all numb.

I slept fitfully through the night. Waking up once to check on Jesus.

I felt an evil magic in the room. When I looked at the clock it said five-oh-five and the phone rang. It rang and rang.

By the time I went to the living room to answer it Jesus was already there. He was sitting next to the phone with his hands clasped before his chest as if he might have been in prayer.

I let it ring two more times before I picked it up.

I was thinking of all the things I would say to her. At one moment I imagined myself screaming, "Whore!" And in the next moment I was breaking down and taking her back. I felt great power and relief lifting the receiver.

I picked up the phone and held it to my ear. I wanted her to say the first words. From her words I could decide what to say.

"Mr. Rawlins?" a man's voice said. "Hello? Anybody there?"

"Who is this?"

"It's Vernor Garnett. Robin's father."

"What you callin' me at this time'a mornin' for?"

"I'm sorry. I'm really sorry. We're just worried, that's all."

Saunders' death and implication in the murders had already been in the paper and the news. They had said that Saunders was killed in a case of self-defense in a barroom brawl in Oakland. Due to the particularly violent nature of the man and due to excellent police work by Quinten Naylor, the man's fingerprints were taken and compared to partial prints left at the scene of the murder of Willa Scott. Saunders was the killer. The killings in Oakland went unknown.

They knew who killed their daughter and they knew that he was dead. Anyway, this man was a prosecuting attorney. What could I know that he couldn't find out?

"What's wrong?" I asked.

"I went down to that hotel where Robin lived. I went to find out about what was happening to her. To find out why."

I felt sorry for the man. To think of a man seeing his daughter lower herself to the squalor of Hollywood Row was an awful thought. I felt it even more because I knew then what it was like to lose a child.

"Mr. Rawlins?"

"I'm listenin', Mr. Garnett. I feel for ya, but that still don't answer why you wanna talk t'me."

"Robin had a baby. At least we think she did."

"What?"

"One of the, uh, people who lived there said that she was pregnant."

"Did he ask you for money?"

"I'm not a fool, Rawlins."

"That don't answer my question."

"He said that he'd tell us about her for twenty dollars and I told him that I'd hear what he had to say before I gave him a dime."

"An' he said she was with child?"

"He gave me the name of the hospital she went to. He took her there."

"Uh-huh." I stifled a yawn.

"We went to the hospital. They hadn't heard of her, but . . ." He hesitated. ". . . but they had done a test on a Cyndi Starr."

"No jive?"

"It was three months ago. She delivered there. I saw the birth certificate. My granddaughter's name is Feather Starr."

I felt the alcohol evaporating out of my pores. A chill climbed my shoulders, and for the first time that I could remember I was completely sober.

"You got this certificate?"

"Right here. Right here in my hand."

"Why you call me?"

"I don't know what to do, Mr. Rawlins. The police say that they'll look into it. We went to see that man Voss. But he told us that the chances are slim. He said that we should keep up hope but that the chances are slim. Hope for this baby is all that my wife has, Mr. Rawlins."

"An' you think I could help where the police cain't?"

"You found us. They say you found the man who killed our daughter."

"Cops tell you that?"

"Yes."

"They tell you to call me?"

"No. We talked it over. We want to hire you if that's okay."

"Hire me for what?"

"Find our granddaughter, Mr. Rawlins. She's all that's left of Robin."

I tried to think about it. But I couldn't. I just opened my mouth and said something. I decided that whatever came out would be what I should do. "I'll be by at around ten, Mr. Garnett. I cain't promise you nuthin'. I cain't promise you a thing, but I'll come on by."

I was at Mofass' office at eight. He was eating jelly doughnuts and sweating even though it wasn't that warm.

He skipped any pleasantries and asked, "You ready fo' me to go to that meetin', Mr. Rawlins?"

"Oh yeah, I'm ready."

"It's set for three-thirty."

"I'll tell ya what, Mofass."

"Yeah?"

"You go tell them boys that we don't need'em."

"What?"

"You heard me. Tell'em I don't give a shit what they want. If we make somethin' outta my places then it's gonna be us to do it."

"Mr. Rawlins, I cain't tell ya what to do with yo' own property, but . . ."

"That's right, man. You ain't got nuthin' t'say about it. It's my money and my life."

"But I promised'em, Mr. Rawlins. I told'em that I could get the partners t'say yeah. You told me you would."

"I never said nuthin' of the kind."

Mofass bit his lower lip, something he hadn't even done when I'd once held a pistol to his head.

"They give me five thousand dollars," he said.

"So?"

"I ain't got it, Mr. Rawlins. I spent it. I thought you was gonna go 'long with'em."

His breathing was getting worse.

"That ain't my problem, William."

"But I took it on your behalf. I took it for our company."

"Shit," was all I had to say.

I left him gagging and coughing in his swivel chair.

The house looked almost the same. The Caddies were still in the driveway but the bicycles were gone. I didn't get a chance to use the buzzer—they had the door open before I was halfway up the walk.

They both came out to meet me. Mr. Garnett shook my hand. He even smiled.

"I'm sorry about the other day, Rawlins. But when I came home Sarah couldn't even talk. Milo was sitting holding her hand and crying."

"Then I guess it's me who should be sorry." I looked at her when I said that.

"Coffee, Mr. Rawlins?" Mrs. Garnett asked.

"Sure, sure," I said.

We sat in the living room again. The couple sat side by side holding hands on the couch. I tried to remember the last time I had been with Regina like that.

"Would you prefer cream?" Mrs. Garnett asked.

"Naw." I looked at them for a few moments more. The man was big and powerful but he was uncertain. He stared at the floor while he patted his wife's hand. She was strength on the verge of collapse. Her brown hair was fading into gray. Her steely blue eyes were in mine, but somewhere else at the same time.

"Can you help us?" she asked.

"Let's see what you got."

The husband had the certificate in an official-looking envelope. It had a cellophane window that revealed a black page that had been scrawled over by a harried hand.

Feather Starr was born on August 12. There was no father mentioned. Back in those days they included race on birth certificates. It was a little box labeled "Race." In Feather's little box there was written a small "w."

"Looks right," I said. "But I thought the paper said that Robin, or Cyndi or whatever you call her, was in Europe until about then?"

"She'd left home about six months ago," Vernor said. "We didn't want to admit it. We were ashamed."

"Did you go to the police?" I asked.

"She was twenty-one, Mr. Rawlins. She told us that she was dropping out of school. The police couldn't have done a thing. What's important now is that we have a granddaughter somewhere." Mr. Garnett had tears in his voice. "It means our baby isn't completely gone."

"Yeah, could be."

"What do you mean?" Mrs. Garnett asked. Her tone of voice was telling me that she might not be able to take one more thing. But I still had things to say.

"Who knows what a girl like this is gonna do with a baby?"

"Girl like what?" the father said.

"You're a prosecutor, man." I looked him right in the eye. "You know what it's like. Fo'them girls money is in their titties and in their legs." I felt myself sneering. Each word hit the man like a haymaker. He winced and cowered in his chair. "A woman up in Hollywood Row be brushin' out her hair for a man to wanna see. He's gonna pay fo'that. One way or the other he gonna pay. Either he gonna buy whiskey while she dancin' on a bar or he gonna hand it over before he walk through the door."

As I spoke I moved toward the edge of my seat. Mr. Garnett folded backwards—he even let go of his wife's hand.

"Why are you doing this?" Mrs. Garnett said. "Why are you torturing him?"

She caught me up short. I sat back to clear my head.

"Just tryin' t'make my point, that's all."

"What point?"

"Girls like the ones live down on the Row live by their bodies. Each piece got its purpose and each piece got its price."

She didn't know what I was talking about, but I was pretty sure that her husband did.

"Baby is just another piece," I said.

"What?"

"Baby got a price tag too. Baby got a big price tag if you know the right market."

"Are you saying that Robin might have sold her baby?" Mr. Garnett's tone was threatening to break out into fists.

"I seen a man pay a woman five dollars so he could put his head on her shoulder."

Garnett leaped to his feet. I didn't flinch though. I didn't flinch because I had a loaded .25 in my pocket.

"Get out my house!" he yelled. "Get out!"

I stood as tall as I could but Vernor still had an inch or two on me.

"All right," I said. "But this is just why I talked like that."

Mrs. Garnett stood and asked, "What do you mean?"

"This thing with yo' girl is ugly and you might not really wanna get into it. You might find out all kindsa things. You might find a dead baby someplace. You might find a pimp done sold your baby girl to some sex fiend in Las Vegas. You open up this can'a worms and you could find out anything. And if you cain't take it then better find out right now."

I felt for them. At least I knew that Regina would take care of my baby. They had one dead child and another one who could be dead or worse.

"You don't have to worry about me, Rawlins," Mr. Garnett said. "I can take whatever I have to."

I believed him. Garnett was large and kind of rugged-looking. His eyes weren't strong but they didn't seem to have much fear either. Like a doctor's eyes when he sees a man dying; just another day.

We were all standing and I didn't want to sit down again. I was afraid to death of sitting down again. I felt that the sadness of that woman would drown me if I stayed any longer.

"Okay, okay," I said. "I'll find the baby if she's there to be found."

"How much?" Mr. Garnett asked.

"I'll take five hundred dollars plus my expense on the day I deliver the baby to you."

Mrs. Garnett saw me to the door. She put her hand on my forearm and looked into my eyes. Her eyes were blue-gray. They shifted back and forth between colors even while I stared into them.

"When should we get in touch with you?" she asked.

"Wait for me. When I know somethin' you'll know it too."

"You're my hope, Mr. Rawlins. I didn't think I could go on until Vernor found out about the baby. If I could just have her."

There was gratitude in her eyes. Gratitude and maybe the desire to go with me.

"I'll call," I said and walked on down the path.

THIRTY THREE

THE TOOTHLESS LAUNDRESS at Lin Chow remembered me right away. She smiled and pulled out a bundle wrapped in brown paper and tied by white string. I paid her a dollar seventy-five and she showed me her gums.

The dirge was plaintive and high, then guttural, an almost human groan. I listened while I went up the stairs and down the hall.

Lips was seated at his table, his chest was bare and his feet were too. He played his horn in a way that would teach any man to love jazz.

The music washed over me like the air at the end of the first battle after D-Day. There were no more bullets or shards of metal flying through the air. The dead lay around in pieces and whole but I couldn't really mourn for them because I was alive. It was pure luck that I wasn't stretched out. I lived a little longer so that I could hurt a little more.

It was a sweet pain.

I sat at the window and listened to him play for a long time. I watched the cars and pedestrians wander while Lips made sense of their lives.

A nice-looking young woman was walking across the street being followed by a pear-shaped man. He was talking loudly and gesturing with his hands. After half a block she stopped and then she smiled. He smiled too. They walked side by side after that. I wondered if they had ever met. Then I wondered if they'd get married.

"What you need now?" Lips asked. I hadn't even realized that he had stopped playing.

"Did you know about her baby?"

"Who baby?"

"Cyndi's." I turned to meet his glassy stare.

"That's why she was gone," he said finally.

"You didn't know?"

"Naw. Not me, man. People go in an' outta here all the time. You know they mo' likely be dead then pregnant."

"Anybody else know her good enough that she might tell them?"

"Sylvia."

"Who's that?"

"I already told you 'bout her. 'Nother white girl. Actress too. Sylvia Bride's what they calls her. I don't know where she is now, though."

"That all?"

"Boy live across the hall from her. Prancer."

"Little guy with a mustache?"

"Uh-huh, they was good friends."

I left twenty dollars on the table and made a note about it in this tiny spiral notepad I'd bought.

The door was unadorned. I knocked for a long time before I heard any sound whatever from inside.

He opened the door wearing crosshatched boxer shorts and brown slippers. His slick hair was tousled and his eyes were bloodshot. He looked at me for a long time trying to think who I might be.

"Yeah?" he said, giving up at last.

"You Prancer?"

"Who're you?"

"Can I come in?"

He stood there a few seconds and then backed up, letting me in the room.

I don't know what I was expecting but the room surprised me. It was very neat, with conservative furnishings, except for the bed. The bed had a wooden headboard painted blue with the figures of little cherubs at the top corners. There was also a sofa and chair set before a coffee table. The coffee table had magazines of various kinds, mainly movie magazines, spread across it.

The only adornment on the wall was a movie poster of James Dean looking tortured and vulnerable.

I sat in the chair and Prancer stood there before me rubbing his eyes. He had the body of a teenaged boy but he must have been in his late twenties, maybe even thirty.

"Do I know you?" he asked.

"I was in Cyndi's room the other day. You wanted me to leave."

"You the cop," he said, suddenly awake and none too pleased.

"Just a man," I said as cool as I could manage. "Lookin' for' somethin'."

"Lookin' fo' what?"

"They say Cyndi had a baby."

"Who says?"

"You told her father that."

Prancer didn't say anything. He just stared at me with his right hand cupped under where his left breast would have been if he were a woman.

"They went to the hospital where you sent them. They found out that Cyndi Starr delivered."

He grinned defiantly and rocked back and forth. "I ain't lied t'them."

"You know where the child is?"

He shook his head like he was shaking water from his hair.

"You know anything could help me find her?"

"How come?"

"Grandparents want the child. It's all they got left."

For a moment Prancer's oblivious child's face showed feeling. "She had a girl?" he asked.

I nodded.

"Listen, man," he said. His face was empty again. "I feel for them, mother and child, but you know I got the rent t'pay. If I got sumpin' t'get you in here wit' me then you know they gotta have some money somewheres."

"I got thirty dollars in my pocket, boy. That's it. Can we deal?"

Prancer actually licked his lips when I laid out the six five-dollar bills in his hand.

"Where?"

"You know Bull Horker?"

It was a question, not an address, but that was all I needed. Much more, actually. Maybe too much.

THIRTY FOUR

BULL HORKER OWNED a ribs-and-chicken joint on the southern outskirts of downtown. It was just an old bungalow that he and his brother owned. They set it on a vacant lot that they leased from a friend who was in jail for manslaughter.

Bull was a massive man. He resembled the sculptures of Balzac done by Rodin. His corpulence was indicative of strength of limb and of spirit. His large gut was a clenched fist. His beefy jowls looked as if they could gnash through pipe.

His skin was mottled like some fine Asian woodwork. It was pulled back tight across his wide, hippopotamus-like face.

"Sylvia who?" he said, cocking his head at such a severe angle that his left ear was almost parallel to the floor.

We were sitting at the back of the dive. The cook, an old ex-convict called Bailey, was frying short ribs and flour behind the counter.

Bull had migrated to Chicago from Mississippi but wound up in L.A. because of his intense dislike of the cold. He did favors for people; so did I. But Mr. Horker's favors always had a price attached up front. Sometimes it was cash; sometimes it was something more dear.

He had plenty of business because he'd do *anything*, from finding a cut-rate engagement ring to killing your worst enemy.

"Sylvia Bride," I said. "That's probably her working name. She does exotic dancing."

"Nope," he smiled. He looked around the room cautiously and then pulled a fifth of some kind of pink liquor from under his chair. "Drink?"

I shook my head no.

"Mind if I try?"

"You sure you don't know her?" I asked again.

"Sure as this here booze." He slugged back a healthy shot. Suddenly there was a powerful odor of apricots.

"The police been lookin' for her in the worst way."

The lizard-skinned clown transformed into a bronze warrior before my eyes. His fists clenched and his jaw set. His eyes became so dull that it was hard to distinguish them from the rest of his face.

"Says which?" he breathed.

"Cops lookin' for this girl, this Sylvia."

"So?"

"They gonna go out t'look in my trail if I cain't locate 'er. We kinda workin' together on this one."

Bull was a big man. I didn't think I would stand a chance against him without a high-caliber gun. As he looked at me I considered my demise. One eye, his left one, nearly shut while the other one opened wide.

I girded myself for the stampede.

Then the right half of his upper lip curled back, revealing an especially feral-looking canine. The rest of his teeth slowly came into view until I saw, with little relief, that Bull was smiling.

"You comin' inta my place an' threatenin' me, Easy Rawlins?"

"I ain't threatenin' nobody. I ain't scared'a you neither. I'm lookin' for this girl and I heard your name. That's all. The police want her. That ain't no threat—it's the truth."

Bull poured another shot of schnapps and drank it.

We had never been at odds before. I wasn't afraid of him any more than I was afraid of any man. The problem wasn't men, it was death.

Death seemed to hound me. He was in Bull Horker's placid visage; he was on a slab in Oakland. She leaned up against a tree a few blocks from my house.

"If I tell you I don't know the girl, then that's all I gotta say," Bull said.

"And if I tell you that somebody got a thousand dollars for something they lost and Sylvia found, then you wouldn't be able to help me, huh?"

Bull just stared.

I wrote my number on the corner of his racing form. Then I walked out of there into the smog and sun of Los Angeles.

Jesus was still at school when I got home. He had emptied out all of my liquor bottles. Poured every one down the drain and set them neatly across the window sill. Even my hundred-dollar bottle of Armagnac.

I took off my clothes and got into the bed.

There was a child crying in my dreams.

THIRTY FIVE

IN THE MORNING I woke to find Jesus asleep at the foot of my bed. He was curled up into a little ball, fully dressed, with his mouth wide open. He was just a little boy and the world around him was whirling like a storm.

I never knew where Jesus was from. For a long time he lived with my friend Primo down in the barrio. But then Primo left for a while and Jesus came to live with me.

I was the closest thing to a father he had, and now that Regina was gone I didn't even come home regularly.

I got up and threw out the bottles that my son had emptied and made breakfast. We had pancakes and bacon. Jesus ate with silent glee.

"Don't worry, boy," I told him. "We're gonna get through this one just like we made it all them other times."

Jesus nodded solemnly. I tickled his ribs and he fell off the chair to the floor.

After he was gone to school I called Quinten Naylor.

"Yes?" he said in my ear.

"Yeah, man. Are you a cop or what?"

"Rawlins?"

"Robin Garnett, Cyndi Starr, or whatever you wanna call'er, had a baby just three months ago. She never went to Europe and she dropped out of UCLA."

He was silent for a moment and then he said, "Go on."

"Viola Saunders said that J.T. was up there when Robin was killed."

"She's just trying to protect him, that's all."

I told him about Prancer and Sylvia.

"We got the killer, Easy."

"You ain't got shit. You just wanna shove yo' head in the dirt and make like it's gonna go away."

Quinten hung up on me and I sat back in my chair.

I wanted a drink. I thought of Regina and slapped myself hard against the head.

Then I called up the memory of the day we buried my mother. It was in St. Ives' graveyard four miles outside of New Iberia, Louisiana. My father wore a black suit and a black tie. He held a spray of honeysuckle in one hand and my hand in the other. My mother's sister and her children were there. The sky was clear and the air was heavy and hot. The minister said a lot of words and my father held my hand. He never let go.

Then, just a week later, he left for logging up in Mississippi. He never came back down. Nobody knew what had happened. Nobody knew a thing. Maybe he died. Maybe he found a new wife and moved away. Maybe he got in a fight one night and killed somebody and he was arrested and sent to jail for the rest of my boyhood.

I sat at the kitchen table and watched the sun edge across it. I watched the floor until I could see the trails of dried mop markings from the last time that Regina had cleaned.

Then I cried. I cried the same misery I had when I was a child. My eyes and nose ran. And I felt my father's hand and an old woman hovering behind me and cried for my loss.

I howled and banged the table. Whenever I let myself feel the pain of that loss I have no fear of Death. I hate him a little. I'd like for him to come meet me outside where I could poke out his eyes.

When it was over my feelings for Regina were gone. At least they weren't yelling in my ears. I still missed Edna like I missed my own childhood, such as it was.

The phone rang just as my breathing returned to normal. It was like a signal.

"Yeah?" I said. I knew that it wasn't Regina. I knew that I'd never hear from her again.

"Mr. Rawlins?"

"Yeah."

"This is Sylvia Bride."

"Uh-huh."

"Can you come up wit' somethin' if I give you the girl?"

"Whose girl is it?"

"Fuck you!"

"That don't tell me nuthin'. I ain't gonna scam nobody. If you could prove it then I might do somethin'. They might too."

She was quiet for a moment. I heard a baby stammer in the silence.

"You know the Beldin Arms?"

"Sure." It was an apartment building on Sixty-third Street.

"Meet me there in an hour."

"What apartment?"

"Just go there," she said and then she hung up.

I dressed casually for the meeting. Tan cotton slacks with a green-and-blue square-cut shirt. I wore sandals without socks. There was a .38 pistol hooked to the back of my belt and a .25 in my pocket.

The phone was ringing when I left but I let it ring. There was nothing so important that it couldn't wait.

I got to the front of the Beldin Arms in exactly one hour. I looked at the mailboxes in the entrance hall, but there was no Sylvia Bride.

While I stood there a small boy ran up the steps. He was short and stocky. He swaggered from side to side as boys are likely to do when they feel important. He seemed to be looking around for accolades on the beautiful job he was doing at playing the child.

He stopped in front of me. "You lookin' fo'a lady?"

"What?" I asked.

"She said you gimme a dollar if I show you."

I handed him a dollar and he started to run out the door, saying over his shoulder, "She in the park."

"What park?"

He waved his right hand indicating the direction and said, "Down there," as if he were talking to a very stupid little brother.

At the end of the block was Beldin Park. Mostly concrete. Four scraggly pines amid a small, balding patch of grass. Sylvia Bride sat on the bench.

She wore red silk pants tapered at the ankle and a red Chinese blouse. Her shoes were powder-blue and her hair could have used some work. It was unwashed and brushed back in bold strokes. She smoked Luckies. There was a half-empty pack in her lap.

"Where's the baby?" I asked, standing above her.

"Sit down." She was quiet and almost demure.

I sat down and asked her, "Where's the baby?"

She took a photograph from inside the cellophane wrapper of the Lucky pack and handed it to me. It was a picture of Cyndi Starr and a small, brown baby.

"I've got a whole album of pictures with them. Any blind fool could see that they're mother and child. I have her diary too. She wrote pages and pages about Feather."

"Is it a daily thing?"

"Huh?"

"Is it a daily journal or is it just about the baby?"

"Oh, no. Cyndi was real smart. She went to college, you know. Every day she'd write down poems and how she felt . . ."

"Is it up to the day she was killed?"

"I don't know. I didn't read it. I mean it was hers."

"But . . ." I began to say and then I held back. No reason to let her realize the book was worth anything.

"I want two thousand dollars. I want it in my hands, and then you can have the baby, the diary, and the album."

I reached for my pocket. "Now lemme see, you want that in tens or twenties?"

She smiled at me. I might have liked Sylvia Bride in another world.

"We could switch. But it has to be someplace safe. And I need two thousand."

"I'll get you the money if I can. We could do it in the zoo or at the beach. I don't care where. But before you see the money my people will have to look at what you got. If that convinces them, then we make the trade."

Sylvia bit her red lips with small, sharp teeth. "Okay," she said. "My number's on the back of that picture. Call me when you find out something."

"Tell me something before you go."

"What?"

"Who killed Cyndi?"

She fumbled for a cigarette. I lit it for her.

"I don't know. It was some crazy man, right?"

"I don't think so. It just doesn't make sense."

"Everybody loved her. She was great."

"Was Bull Horker a friend of hers too?"

"He let her stay at his place down near Redondo while she was pregnant. But that's all."

"He the father?"

"God knows who the father is, Mr. Rawlins."

"How was she living when she couldn't work?"

"She borrowed from Bull. But he didn't do it. She was going to pay him three thousand dollars."

"From where?"

"I don't know, honey. She said that she was going to get it from some man."

"A white man?"

"She never said. I mean . . ." Sylvia stopped talking and turned her head at an angle.

"She said," Sylvia continued, "that she didn't like somebody but that they had to pay up."

We both let that one sit until she got up to go.

"Why you come to me, Sylvia?" I said.

"You came to me. You're the one."

"But you could have called that girl's parents yourself. You could do it now."

"I'm not talking to white people about this," she said.

I'd heard that all the time. Half the black people I knew would walk an extra mile to avoid straightforward contact with white people. It didn't surprise me that white people might not trust each other. I couldn't trust them, so why should they trust each other?

Sylvia crossed the street and walked down the block. At the end of the street she got into the passenger's seat of a new Ford. I thought I knew who the driver was.

THIRTY SIX

JESUS AND I went to Pecos Bob's Barbecue Heaven for dinner. He had two servings of ribs. Then we went to the penny arcade at the Santa Monica pier. He played the little coin games and rode the merry-go-round. It was great fun.

I bought a beer but didn't drink it. Jesus had cotton candy and caramel corn, but that was okay, he needed to feel good. We went home feeling dizzy from the red flashing lights and bells.

He was kind of slow in the morning but at least he slept in his own bed. I watched him trail off toward school. He met up with two little girls from across the street. I never even knew that Jesus had friends he walked to school with.

Mrs. Garnett was home.

"Two thousand dollars?" she gasped.

"That's what she said. But first you get to see the diary, the photo album with all the pictures of Cyn—of Robin and her baby."

I didn't mention that the baby was black. Many times little black babies look white when they're born. The color sets in later on. I figured I'd let the shock of race set in on them without my trying to soften it. After all, a black baby didn't bother me.

"I don't know. I'll have to talk to my husband."

"Okay. I'll call you tonight. But if he says yeah, then how long before you get the money?"

"I don't know if he will agree."

"But if he does?"

She hesitated but then said, "Day after tomorrow, maybe."

I spent the day cleaning up. I threw Regina's things away. She'd left clothing and costume jewelry and knickknacks all over the house. I threw all of that out. Edna's toys and blankets, those that were left, I piled in her crib. I covered all of that with a big blanket and left it in the living room.

I spent the afternoon reading *The Souls of Black Folk* by W.E.B. Du Bois. It was a book Jackson Blue told me about years before.

Jesus came home at about three-thirty and we played catch until six. We had pork chops, mashed potatoes with sautéed onions, and canned asparagus for dinner. After that Jesus split a candy bar with me and I asked him to wash the dishes.

The phone rang at eight o'clock.

"Hello."

"Mr. Rawlins. My wife tells me that you've found our baby."

"Maybe, sir. I don't know. Woman had a picture of your daughter and a little baby. She says that she's got an album full of enough pictures to prove to anybody that it's your granddaughter."

"What's this woman's name and what does she have to do with Robin?"

"She was Robin's friend. Her name is Sylvia."

"Sylvia what?"

"You not gonna find her in any phone book, Mr. Garnett."

"But maybe I know her. If she was my daughter's friend I might know her."

"Bride," I said. "Sylvia Bride."

"No. I never heard that name before. You say she wants two thousand dollars?"

"She said that."

"It's a lot of money for something we don't even know for sure."

"Listen," I said. "I'll call her and make a meeting where she will show you the book. If you think the baby in the pictures is the daughter, then you can make a deal. You don't have to bring the money with you. Leave it with your lawyer. I'll call her after this an' say that we all gonna meet tomorrow at four on the front stairs of the main library downtown. Okay?"

"My wife said something about a diary."

"Yeah. It seems like she did a lot of writing about Feather. Sylvia seems to think that it will help to identify the baby." I paused for a moment.

"Listen, Mr. Garnett. I don't think that that crazy man killed your girl."

"What?"

"I can't go into all of it right now but I think that somebody killed her and made it seem like she was the crazy man's victim."

"But nobody knew about the crazy man until after she was dead."

"People all over my neighborhood did. Some of them might even have found out about those burns."

"It doesn't sound likely, Mr. Rawlins. That's all pretty elaborate."

"She was seen with some man the day she was killed. And Sylvia told me that somebody was going to give Cyndi some money. Maybe this diary will tell us who that is."

"My God," Garnett said. He sounded so broken up that I felt sorry I had confided in him. There was enough pain in his life.

After a long minute he said, "I hope you're wrong. I hope . . . Well, nothing to do but meet this woman and see what she's got."

"You sure now?"

"Yes. Yes, I'm certain."

"All right. Then I'll call her an' make the date. If sumpin' happens I'll call you back, all right?"

He took a deep breath and then said, "Okay."

Sylvia was unhappy at first. But I told her that she didn't have to have the baby there. All she had to have was the photographs and the diary. The library was as public and safe as she was about to get.

Jesus went to sleep early and was off to school before I was out of bed.

I was working in the garden around noon when Quinten Naylor and Roland Hobbes drove up in front of my house. They walked abreast and each of them gave me a noncommittal stare.

"Ezekiel Rawlins . . ." Roland Hobbes started the speech.

"Hold it, man," I said. "Lemme get a call on the phone before you take me down. My wife is gone and my little boy is mute. Lemme call somebody down here 'fore you take me in."

Hobbes and Naylor exchanged glances. Neither one of them

said a thing. Finally Naylor nodded and Hobbes accompanied me to the telephone.

"Hola," said Flower. Her voice was deep and dark as a South American rain forest. Even listening to her brought images of large white lilies on a black bough. I could hear children in the background. The children Jesus called brother and sister before he came to live with me.

I told her to send Primo, her husband, up for the boy. I told her that I was going to jail. She gave me a friendly sigh of sorrow and said okay. The thought that I still had a friend in the world lightened my heart a little.

I hung up the phone and Roland Hobbes said, "Ezekiel Rawlins, you are under arrest."

They didn't tell me a thing. Just cuffed me and drove me down to the station house.

They put me in a holding cell, where I sat until seven-thirty the next morning. It wasn't much of a cell. It was more like a high-ceilinged hopper room with a chair and a light fixture. There were no windows, nor even bars. Just a gray room with a chair. They took my cigarettes, so I was edgy.

There was an eye hole in the gray metal door. Every once in a while it seemed to darken a little, as if someone were looking in at me.

Two uniformed cops came to escort me to court. I met my court-appointed lawyer before the bench. I didn't catch his name. He didn't shake my hand.

Then my lawyer and the prosecution went to the bench and talked with the judge. They discussed my fate for thirty seconds and my lawyer came back to where I stood.

He was a sandy-haired, short man with ears that stood straight away from his head. He was middle-aged and skinny but he still had bad posture and shirttails that brimmed out of his pants.

"What's this all about?" I asked him.

He shuffled his papers together and walked away from the desk. The judge said, "Next case," just like on television, and the court officers started to hustle me off.

I grabbed at my lawyer's jacket.

"Lemme talk to my man a minute," I begged.

"What do you want, Mr. Rawlins?" the little lawyer, whose name I never knew, asked.

"What am I in here for an' what happens now?"

"You're in here for extortion, Mr. Rawlins, and you go to jail until somebody posts twenty-five thousand dollars or your trial comes up."

The lawyer turned away and I was dragged to a room where four other men slept. A half an hour later the sleeping men were roused by three court officers.

We were hustled into a bus that had wire mesh over all the windows and a cell door separating us from the driver. He didn't need that protection, though, because each of the prisoners was manacled by his handcuffs to a bolt under his seat.

We were driven to a flat building near the southern outskirts of town.

The building we were taken to wasn't originally a jail. Maybe they made ball bearings there, or apricot jam. The walls were made of concrete, probably reinforced with steel.

The prisoners were led to a large room, half a football field in size. In the middle of the big room the state had erected steel cages. Like the cages in the older zoos. There looked to be forty-five or fifty of the cells. About half of them were occupied.

One cage to a man. Each one was eight by eight by eight and furnished with a small cot. There were two pails on the floor. One had a cup to drink from, the other was there when you needed to relieve yourself.

One of the other prisoners sold me a pack of cigarettes for a five-dollar bill that I had palmed before leaving the house. When the guards were gone and I was safely locked away, I lit up.

I still remember how good that cigarette tasted. As bad as my life had turned in those few days I still remember that moment as being one of the most satisfying in my life.

For a while the new inmates talked to the old ones. I asked the guy in the cell next to mine, "What kinda jail is this?"

"Temporary," the gray old white man said. "They're buildin' a new one and this is just the overflow."

I handed him a cigarette and lit it.

"Obliged," he said.

Then the guards told us to be quiet.

Somebody might not believe what happened to me. They might say that a prisoner in America always knows the specific crime of which he is accused. They might say that a man has a right to good counsel and at least a phone call.

At one time I would have said that white people had those rights but colored ones didn't. But as time went by I came to understand that we're all just one step away from an anonymous grave. You don't have to live in a communist country to be assassinated; just ask J.T. Saunders about that.

The police could come to your house today and drag you from your bed. They could beat you until you swallow teeth and they could lock you in a hole for months.

I knew all that but I put it far out of my mind. I just lay back on my cot and savored the cigarette.

THIRTY SEVEN

I WAS IN the cell but I wasn't alone. Naylor, Voss, Violette, and Hobbes were in there with me.

Naylor said, "You didn't want to help a black woman but you go out for some white whore."

"I saw you with her," Hobbes said.

Voss just shook his head and spit.

Then Violette unholstered his pistol. When he cocked back the hammer it made a squeaking sound instead of a crack.

Then I hear, outside of the dream, "Look out, boy!" And then I felt a cold spray against my face. Another voice curses but by that time I'm doubling up from the cot.

He went past me, driving the knife he held into the mattress rather than into me. His body was over mine and I gave him an uppercut to the groin that would have halted a gorilla.

My attacker fell to the floor, huffing and coughing. It was a white man in a gray jail suit. I kicked him once in the ribs and then I stamped my foot down on his right hand. I was barefoot and so could feel his fingers snapping along with the pain in my heel.

I broke his hand so I wouldn't have to kill him. I had to do something. I would have been within my rights, as I see them, to kill a killer. But instead I disabled him.

I picked him up and dragged him down the aisle of cages and threw him on the floor in front of the door that led to the guards' kiosk. As I went back toward my cell a commotion began among the waking prisoners. By the time I'd locked myself away there were seven guards stumbling over the would-be killer.

He was holding his hand over his groin and coughing. The guards looked around suspiciously.

I noticed a very sour odor. I wondered if it was my own fear that I smelled.

"He's got keys!" one of the guards shouted.

"Pssst!"

The man yelled in pain as they pulled him from the floor. I felt my toe and realized that I had probably broken his rib too.

"Pssst!" It was the old white man next to me.

I looked at him and he smiled. He was missing teeth both upper and lower.

"Hope I didn't get your cigarettes with that piss." His smile broadened and I realized that he was the one who'd warned me, who'd thrown water—urine—in my face.

He giggled and said, "Lucky there warn't no turds in there."

It struck me as so funny that I had to laugh, but I couldn't laugh because that would have called attention from the guards, who were looking around for somebody to brutalize.

I sat there with tears coming from my eyes and my diaphragm beating against my chest. When the guards went past my cell I covered myself with the blanket to keep them from smelling the guilt. The foul odor made me gag harder.

After a while the guards took that groaning assassin away.

"You got a good friend somewhere," the old white man said. He wore jail gray also.

"What do you mean?"

"Somebody went to a lotta trouble to kill you." He gave me a wink. "Unless you know that bozo."

I handed my savior five cigarettes.

"What's your name?" I asked him.

"Alamo. Alamo Weir." He winked at me and I lit his cigarette.

I lay back in the squalor and began to think. I started with Quinten Naylor coming up to my house and driving me to the scene of a crime.

They fitted me with jailhouse grays the next morning. We all went into a big room with a long table and ate thick oatmeal watered down with reconstituted milk. At midday they let us walk around outside of our cells. During that time Alamo stuck with the white prisoners and I moved with the colored brothers.

After we were back in our cells I was taken to a room where Anthony Violette was waiting for me.

"Glad to see that you're still alive, Rawlins." He smiled at me.

I couldn't say a word. A police captain wanted me dead. I was dead.

"No smart-assed joke? Maybe you could go get me a beer."

"I ain't done nuthin' this bad to you, man," I said.

"That's right. You haven't done a damn thing to me. I'm just a police officer, doing my duty."

"What am I in here for?"

"Extortion." Violette's smile was plastered to his face. The humiliation he felt from me was immense. One black man talking back to him in front of a superior; maybe that was enough to have me killed.

"I didn't extort anybody."

"That's not what Vernor Garnett says."

"He killed her." It jumped right out of my mouth. It was so fast and so natural that the smile was blasted from Violette's face.

"What?"

"He killed his own daughter and now he's using you and me to cover his track."

"Listen here, Rawlins . . ."

"No. You listen to me. Vernor was supposed to meet me yesterday afternoon in front of the main library. A woman who knew about Cyndi's daughter was going to bring proof that the baby was Cyndi's."

"What kind of proof? What baby?" the cop asked in spite of himself.

"A bunch'a pictures and a diary that might have identified the killer, the man who was going to bring her three thousand dollars."

"Who're you? Charlie Chan?"

"What'd he say I did?"

"What you did do. You threatened to go to the papers about his daughter. You were going to expose her life down in Watts."

"I bet that's what *she* did. I bet she was going to tell the family about her life and her daughter too. Yeah. He already knew about the baby."

"You're crazy, Rawlins. She didn't have a kid. And Vernor didn't know about her before you told him."

"She did have a baby. She'd left home and had it at one of Bull Horker's places."

He hadn't believed a word up until I mentioned Horker.

"Where were you going to meet this girl?" The cop was fully in charge now.

I told him my story again. He didn't tell me a thing. When I was finished he just stood up, in a hurry to leave.

"What about me?" I asked him.

"Come up with the bail."

"But I didn't extort nuthin'."

"That's what you say. Maybe you just read the papers. We'll see."

"Listen, captain," I said in a voice loud enough to stop him a moment. "There's somebody trying to kill me in here."

Violette's grin came back for a surprise visit. "He wasn't going to kill you, Rawlins. He was going to stick you in the shoulder and twist a little. That's all. You know, you need a little lesson."

Alamo and I shared a few cigarettes that he got and sat up all that night. He was a career criminal. He'd done everything, if you were to believe him, from petty larceny to first-degree murder.

He'd been born in a small town in Iowa and hit the road after he was let loose from the army after World War I.

"It just warn't never right after that. All them dead boys," Alamo told me. He shook his head in real remorse. "And all them people, never felt it, act like they know life. Damn. I could take their money or their life. They wouldn't even know it was gone."

He was kind of crazy but I was comforted by him. After all, it was sane men who had put me in jail.

The next morning the guard came and took me from the cell. Alamo had passed me a sharpened spoon in the night, and I had it up the long sleeve of my gray jail shirt. We walked along the big tables and out through large double doors that led to a garage.

The guard told me to pick up a box that sat in a corner. I looked down in it to see my civilian clothes.

"Put 'em on," the porky, crew-cut white man said.

I stripped right there in front of him, carefully leaving the spoon in the sleeve of the shirt. After I was dressed in my normal clothes I threw the prison garb into a corner and retrieved my weapon.

Another guard came up and they escorted me to the driveway in front of the factory. There sat a squad car with two cops in it. The cops got out and put manacles on me, hand and foot.

"Where'm I goin'?" I asked once.

The police just laughed.

I sat in the backseat on the way downtown. Every moment was very important. I looked at windows with manikins in them and got weepy. I saw a man make a left turn and I imagined myself turning the steering wheel. I thought of my baby girl and felt my inner organs shift.

It must have taken an hour to drive all the way downtown but it seemed like fleet moments to me. They hustled me out of the car and then put me in another holding cell. I was sure that someone was going to kill me. I had the spoon hidden in my pocket. I didn't think that I could fight past guns with that spoon, but I could take somebody with me; at least I could do that.

In the afternoon they took me from the holding cell and brought me to a wire-cage kiosk. A young cop pushed a big manila envelope at me. Inside it I found my wallet and keys. Those simple items scared me so much that I began to tremble. I knew that I was being set up for the kill.

I walked out of the front door of the municipal building next to city hall with my shoulders hunched and my head down.

"Easy!" he yelled.

I looked up, ready to go down fighting, only to see Raymond Alexander in all his splendor. He wore a close-fitting bright checkered jacket and flared black slacks. He shoes were ivory and his hat close-brimmed. Mouse smiled for miles.

"You look terrible," he said.

"What you doin' here, Raymond?"

"I done made yo' bail, Easy. I got you out."

"What?"

"Com'on, man, let's get outta here. Them cops prob'ly take us in fo'loiterin' fo'long."

In the car we went past the squat buildings of fifties L.A. down into Watts.

"Where you wanna go, Easy?" Mouse asked after a while.

"You came up with my bail?"

"Uh-huh."

"Twenty-five hundred dollars?"

"Uh-uh. Twenty-five thousand. Bail bondsman wouldn't touch it."

"Where you come up wit' money like that? You go to Mofass?"

"Tried to but he's in the hospital."

"Hospital?"

"Yeah. Some white boys tore him up. He told me to tell you that them men you been doin' business wit' is mad in the worst way."

"Shit. So where'd you get the money?"

"You sure you wanna know?" He was smiling.

"Where?"

"There's this private poker game out in Gardena. I robbed it."

"An' they had that much money?"

"An' some to boot."

"You kill anybody?"

"Shot this one guy but I don't think he gonna die. Maybe just walk funny fo'awhile."

THIRTY EIGHT

BULL HORKER WAS found in an alley in San Pedro. He'd been shot seven times in the chest. The police believed that he was killed somewhere else and dumped in that alley. He was found at eight P.M. on the day I was supposed to meet Sylvia and Vernor on the library steps.

The article said that there were signs of a struggle but there was no explanation of what the signs were.

Primo and Flower were glad to see us. Jesus was so happy I thought he might even talk. He ran up and put his arms around me and he just wouldn't let go. I had to walk with his embrace and sit with him on my lap.

Mofass looked pretty good in his hospital bed. The rest gave him a little strength and they wouldn't let him smoke in the ward. His only problems were a busted hand and three fractures in his left leg.

"They th'owed me down the steps, Mr. Rawlins. They didn't care if I was dead. They told me that if I lived I should tell my partners that they ain't playin'."

Mouse grinned.

"I'll take care of it, William. You just rest here and try to give up them cigars. You know they gonna kill you faster than DeCampo."

"It's killin' me *not* to smoke."

I gave Mouse the names of DeCampo and his associates. I told him their Culver City office address and asked him to visit each and every one of them, on the most private terms.

"I want them to understand that killing Mofass won't save their lives," I said. "And, Raymond," I pointed in his face, "I don't want nobody dead or even wounded."

I've read many a novel that extolled the virtues of capitalism. Not one of them ever came within a mile of the truth.

I was sitting at my desk in the early evening going over the accounts of the killing of Bull Horker. I was looking for something that might lead me to Vernor. But there was nothing I could see.

I was already used to the silence. The silence we'd lived with before Regina, and then Edna. Jesus was reading a red storybook. And I was still alive.

Then the screech of the gate brought me to the window. There was Quinten Naylor again. He was wearing the same suit he wore the day he brought me to see Bonita Edwards' body.

I blamed him for Regina leaving me. I blamed him but I knew I was wrong.

He wasn't surprised to see me open the door before he could knock. I nodded at a chair that stood where the crib had been and he sat down.

I lit a cigarette. He brushed his hand over the top of his head.

"The charges against you have been dropped," Naylor said.

"Oh? How come?"

"They got the wife in custody."

"What about Milo?" That little boy was the first one I thought of.

"Juvenile Hall."

"Yeah. Take it out on the kid. Put him in jail 'cause'a what his old man did."

"His mother was in on it. She confessed."

"What? Naw, I don't believe it. I saw how she acted when I showed her the pictures."

"She didn't know then. But after that she began to put things together. Garnett had told her something about the killings before their daughter was killed. She didn't think anything until after he told her about their granddaughter. He'd been in touch with Robin even after she'd left school. He had to know that she was pregnant."

"So she found out when he was planning to go after Sylvia?"

"He was scared over the diary. Robin had threatened to come to his office dressed like a whore and with a baby in her arms if he didn't give her enough money to care for her child."

"Killed his own child." I was saddened by even the possibility.

"She drove him to it," Quinten said. "She was a whore and she just wouldn't straighten out. Then she threatened him."

"She drove him to it," I said. "Well then, what drove her?"

Quinten didn't understand the question. There was right and wrong for him. He dealt with morality the way Mofass went after money. There is no such thing as a long-term investment, there's money right now, there's sin right now. Mofass didn't see past the money those crooks blinded him with and Quinten Naylor couldn't see that maybe Vernor Garnett had sown the seeds of his own destruction.

"Where is the father?" I asked.

"He ran after going to meet Sylvia. He killed Bull Horker, we're pretty sure of that. Then he disappeared with the girl. We found his car in West Hollywood yesterday. Bull's blood was all over the front seat."

"What happened to the girl?"

"Nothing yet. All we know is what I said. His name and picture are out there. We'll get him."

"I'm sure of that."

"What's that supposed to mean?"

"You're good at gettin' people, Quinten. You got J. T. Saunders good. When Violette thought I mighta done somethin' he had me set up faster than you could spit."

"What are you talking about, Rawlins? When a prosecutor says that someone is extorting him we believe it. Especially when . . ."

"When it's a nigger. Especially then. Yeah. What are you doing here anyway, man? You gonna me send down to jail again?"

Naylor studied a few fingernails before he answered. "I wanted to say I'm sorry." The words seemed to stick in his mouth. "I always thought that . . . I don't know. I just always thought that I could work inside the police and keep my hands clean. I put myself above you. Don't get me wrong, I'm not saying that I think you live right. But maybe I'm not so much better."

Maybe Naylor wasn't so bad either. I didn't tell him that, though. I didn't tell him a thing.

THIRTY NINE

OVER THE NEXT few days things came back into order, after a fashion. Anybody who asked me was told that Regina had gone to visit her sick aunt in Arkansas.

Jack DeCampo came to Mofass' hospital room—to apologize. He blamed the attack on *silent partners* and said that he didn't know about the mayhem until it was already too late.

Mofass didn't want to let him off at first but he remembered the kind of fear that Mouse could throw into a man.

"You know, Mr. Rawlins," Mofass told me on the phone, "that man was so pale that he could a been two white men."

It was rare that Mofass and I laughed at the same joke.

"When I told'im that our friend was on the payroll and that he didn't have to be scared I thought he mighta kissed me."

"Okay, William," I said. "Maybe next time you'll fly right."

"Uh-huh. But you know there is this one thing."

"What?"

"They still wanna be partners. They say they'll give a hunnert an' twenty-five thousand just to be twenty-five percent." He was making deals from what might have been his deathbed.

"Man . . ."

"They got good connections, Mr. Rawlins. They could get us deals that no bank ever gonna give a Negro."

The thought of DeCampo working for me sounded good. And I could use the cash for development.

"You tell'im eighteen percent and he's got a deal."

"Okay, man." I could hear his grin over the phone.

The telephone rang four days after Quinten Naylor's visit. I still got butterflies whenever I had to answer a phone. I still thought, What can I say to her?

"Hello?"

"Is this a Mr. Rawlins?" a young man's voice said.

"Yeah."

"Well . . . I don't know, sir. This is kinda weird."

"What's that?"

"Well, you see this couple . . . have been eating here at the Chicken Pit for about a week now."

The butterflies were beating up a storm.

"And a couple of days ago the woman, just a girl really, comes up from the table to ask me for a glass of water. But when she reaches for the glass she grabs my finger and passes this note. I think she was worried . . ."

"What did this note say?"

"It was a corner of a newspaper, a racing form with your name and phone number in one margin and a note saying, 'Call the police, we're at the Seacrest,' and it's signed 'Sylvia.' "

"Why'd you wait two days, man?"

"I don't know. It was just so weird. I don't want any trouble. You see . . . I can't talk to the police."

"Where's this Seacrest place?"

"It's a motel at the corner of Adams and La Brea. Do you think . . ."

"Have they been in your place since then?"

"The next day I had off. I went to San Diego and really forgot about . . ."

"Was she in there today?"

"No. Just the man, I mean. That's why I called."

I hung up the phone and rushed to the closet to get my gun.

Jesus followed me around the house and kept grabbing me. Finally I stopped and asked him, "What?"

He just stared at the pistol in my hand.

"It's not Regina," I told him. "She's gone. It's not her."

At first Jesus didn't believe me. But I sat down and convinced him after a while. I told him that I'd be back soon. Then I drove off in the direction of the Seacrest.

At every red light I tried to persuade myself to call the cops. On every straightaway I imagined killing Vernor Garnett. He was everything I hated. He'd killed his own child and his wife still stayed behind him. He'd got me in jail by just telling a lie. A white man.

The Seacrest was a single-story motel facing a large parking lot with the entrances to all of the rooms facing out. I parked across the street at three in the afternoon and waited.

I sat there for three hours. And the whole time all I thought about was Regina. I'd tried to think about her before but all I encountered was pain. But somehow, waiting for that evil man, I didn't feel the pain. I only felt cold rage.

By the time Garnett walked out of the last room on the end I hadn't figured out a thing. I couldn't say for a fact why she left me. I couldn't say that I would have been different.

Garnett had grown some facial hair and wore a trench coat with the lapels turned up. He walked down the street to the Chicken Pit with his head down.

I jimmied his door and went in.

Sylvia was dead. He'd laid her out on the floor of the closet and closed the door. But she was already starting to smell. Her temple was caved in. The room was a shambles. Clothes and bags of food were thrown around. A newspaper spread on the bed was open to the travel section. Three special fares to Mexico were circled.

I turned out the light and stood behind the door. I just waited there forever. The gray forms of the bed and dressser got fainter. The pistol was cold on my fingers.

When Garnett came back he opened the door and closed it before flicking on the light. I hadn't expected to be blinded by the sudden light.

"What," Vernor called out loudly as if maybe he was with somebody. But he was alone.

Maybe if he had jumped me in that second I would have been keeping Sylvia company. But instead he clawed at the doorknob for two seconds, three.

I flat-handed him with the pistol. He shook his head as if assailed by a sudden and unpleasant memory. I hit him again and he went down to his knees like J. T. Saunders had done for the police assassin.

"Please," he said in a small voice.

A voice was screaming in my head, "Kill him!" Over and over. My neck quivered. I honestly felt that if I didn't pull the trigger I would die. The tears came from my eyes, a guttural cry escaped my lips. My diaphragm undulated so that it was hard to keep the pistol steady.

Garnett cowered against the door. He held his hands up before his face. We were both madmen at the end of our lives. We were madmen but only he was a lawyer.

He started talking. At first I was too upset to hear him but then after a while his gibbering began to make sense. He told me that he didn't mean it. He hadn't planned to kill his daughter. But after he had, he faked Saunder's MO, because he'd heard about it down at the courthouse.

He had killed her in his car also.

"What about Sylvia?"

"I just wanted the diary," he pleaded. "They didn't bring it with them."

"Why'd you kill her?"

"It was too late," he said. "She wouldn't give me. She wanted . . . wanted . . ."

I hog-tied Garnett and gagged him; put him in the closet with Sylvia Bride.

"Hello?" Quinten Naylor said.

I gave him the address and told him that somebody had called. I didn't know who.

Maybe to some people revenge is sweet. All I know is that I had to stop my car five blocks away and vomit for a full minute before I could breathe again.

Bull Horker's cook, Bailey, was more than happy to tell me where Cyndi stayed in Redondo Beach. For another fifty dollars he would have shed blood for me.

The house on Exeter was inhabited by an old woman named

Charla Fine. She was holding the baby for Bull Horker and she was none too happy that the Bull had died. But Feather seemed hale and more or less happy. When I first saw her she was sucking her toe. I looked down and she smiled at me and said something in baby talk that I thought meant "Tickle my stomach and push my nose."

Five hundred dollars and the baby was mine.

The papers the next day detailed the crime. The dead stripper Sylvia Bride (her real name was Phyllis Weinstein) had her picture on the front page all over California.

The trial was front-page news for weeks. Everything the prosecutor wanted to avoid came out in public. His daughter's wild life, and death. The father's crime, the mother's cover-up.

Nobody cared much about the baby. Most of the speculation was that the child had probably been killed by the mother. This was substantiated by the fact that no one had seen the baby after she was born.

Anyway, the birth certificate had the baby listed as white. Feather was safe with me.

Vernor Garnett died in prison two years after he was sentenced. His wife moved back east somewhere after she was found innocent of conspiracy.

There wasn't much written about Milo.

FORTY

WE MOVED THREE months later. I bought a small house in an area near West Los Angeles called View Park. Middle-class black families had started colonizing that neighborhood, and I wanted to get away from people who knew me and Regina.

Jesus liked his new school, and all the work of moving got my mind off the trouble in my life. Regina still lived in my dreams. Sometimes I'd wake up in the middle of the night in despair.

But when I'd wake up, little Feather needed her bottle and a change of diapers. She wasn't my little Edna but she was beautiful and happy almost all of the time. I'd lost Regina and Gabby Lee, but Jackson Blue would baby-sit at least once a week and I didn't mind caring for her.

Jesus never got tired of playing with Feather. He'd take her everywhere once she started to walk.

And I decided to let Dupree and Regina leave for good.
Mouse found out where they had gone. He offered to go down to
kill Dupree, and Regina, and bring Edna back. But I told him to
give me the address and let it lie.

Enough people had died. I would have been happy if not one
more person in the world ever had to face that fate.